THE FAMOUS FIVE VERSUS THE BLACK MASK

THE FAMOUS FIVE are Julian, Dick, George (Georgina by rights), Anne and Timmy the dog.

A Mediterranean cruise on the liner *North Wind* is an exciting prospect for the Five and their friend Tinker.

Then a series of thefts confirms a rumour that the famous international

Then a series of thefts confirms a rumour that the famous international criminal is on board! Who, out of all the innocent-looking passengers, can the thief be? The children are determined to find out before the end of the holiday!

Also available in Knight Books:

The Famous Five Versus the Black Mask

A new adventure of the
characters created by
Enid Blyton, told by Claude
Voilier, translated by
Anthea Bell

Illustrated by John Cooper

KNIGHT BOOKS
Hodder and Stoughton

British Library C.I.P.

Voilier, Claude
    The Famous Five versus the
    Black Mask—(Knight Books)
    I. Title   II. Les Cinq contre le
    Masque Noir. *English*
843'.914[J]   PZ7

ISBN 0-340-27864-1

Printed and bound in Great Britain
for Hodder and Stoughton
Paperbacks, a division of Hodder
and Stoughton Ltd., Mill Road,
Dunton Green, Sevenoaks, Kent
TN13 2YA (Editorial Office: 47
Bedford Square, London WC1B
3DP) by Richard Clay Ltd.,
Bungay, Suffolk.

CONTENTS

Chapter One

A VERY EXCITING HOLIDAY

'Go on, where do you think we're going to spend our holidays this summer? I bet you'll never guess!'

George Kirrin looked challengingly at her cousins. George's real name was Georgina, but she had always wished she was a boy instead of a girl, and she did look very like one, with her short curly hair and blue jeans.

Her inseparable companion, Timmy the dog, was sitting beside her. He too was looking at the others as if he were waiting for them to reply!

Julian, Dick and Anne looked at each other, intrigued. They were wondering what George could mean. They had just arrived at Kirrin Cottage, the home of George's parents, Uncle Quentin and Aunt Fanny, expecting to spend the summer there as usual. And now it seemed they were going somewhere else!

'Why – do Uncle Quentin and Aunt Fanny want to get rid of us?' joked Dick. He was eleven, like George, and in fact, as they were both dark and lively, they looked rather like each other.

'No,' said George, laughing, 'my parents are coming with us!'

Julian, a fair-haired boy who was very tall for thirteen, shook his head.

'Coming with us where?' he said. 'I'm no good at guessing games, George! Anyway, I don't see where we *could* be going except for Kirrin!'

'Nor do I,' said Anne. She was ten, and the youngest of the children. 'I've no idea at all.' Timmy barked, and Anne gave him a loving smile. She was so pleased to see dear old Timmy again! Pushing her fair hair back from her forehead, she said, 'As long as we're all together it doesn't matter *where* we go! Do you mean Aunt Fanny and Uncle Quentin are taking us on a trip to a seaside resort? Or perhaps we're going to the Welsh mountains again? Am I getting warm, George?'

'No, you're still stone cold!' George's eyes were sparkling.

Her cousins were baffled. 'Well, *where*, then?' asked Julian. 'Going to the moon, are we? Or down underground somewhere?'

'No – on the water!'

'A fishing holiday!' cried Dick.

'Even better! A cruise in the Mediterranean!

8

Your mother and father wanted it to be a surprsie for you, so they sent your passports on here to us without telling you about the plan! Well – what do you think of *that*?'

The other three were simply stunned for a moment! Then they burst into shouts of delight.

'How thrilling! We're going on a cruise – hurray!' cried Dick enthusiastically. 'Where exactly are we going?'

George went on explaining. 'Except that it's in the Mediterranean, we shan't know till we get there! It's going to be a mystery cruise – the passengers won't be told where the liner stops, until just before it gets there. The ship is called the *North Wind* – a real luxury liner! It was my mother's idea.'

Julian was rather surprised. 'But didn't Uncle Quentin mind? I can't see him agreeing to leave his beloved work at home! He's so wrapped up in his books and his scientific calculations he never thinks of anything else!'

'That's just why we're going,' George told her cousin. 'You see, he's been overworking, and for once my mother put her foot down! She wants to take him right away from his books and papers, for a real rest. She thought he wouldn't be tempted to work at sea.'

George stopped for a moment, with a mischievous look on her face, and then started chuckling.

'But I'll tell you something else – I don't think my

father *will* have that rest after all! I'm sure he's only agreed to come on the cruise because Professor Hayling is going to be there too.'

Like Uncle Quentin, Professor Hayling was a famous scientist, and his son, whose nickname was Tinker, was one of the children's best friends.

'Is Tinker coming as well?' asked Anne.

'Yes, of course! And what's more, animals are allowed on board the *North Wind*. So Timmy can come too, and Tinker can bring his little monkey Mischief!'

'That's very good news!' said Julian.

'Yes,' said Dick. 'I bet you wouldn't have come without Timmy, George!'

'No, I certainly wouldn't!' agreed George. 'I can't bear being parted from my dog.'

'And without you and Timmy we wouldn't be the Five!' said Dick, smiling.

What he meant was that the four cousins and Timmy called themselves the Five – the Five loved solving mysteries, and had had all sorts of exciting times together. But never one quite like this before!

'I wonder if there'll be an adventure on this cruise?' Dick went on. 'Do you think there'll be a puzzle, or a mystery or something for us to clear up?'

'Well, why not?' said George. 'Anything could happen! But in any case, we certainly shan't be bored on a Mediterranean cruise!'

Julian, Dick and Anne were delighted at the idea

of the good time they were going to have. When they arrived at Kirrin Cottage they hadn't had an inkling of the exciting holiday in store!

'We leave for Southampton the day after tomorrow,' George added. 'Tomorrow we must decide what summer clothes to take with us. I expect my mother will help us pack! Now, why don't we go and see Tinker? I bet he's as pleased as we are.'

Ten minutes later, the children were riding the beautiful new bicycles Uncle Quentin had given them along the road to the village of Big Hollow, followed by Timmy, who was glad of a chance to stretch his legs properly. Professor Hayling and Tinker lived in Big Hollow house, a few miles from Kirrin and near Demon's Rocks, where the Five had had an exciting adventure not so long ago.

Tinker was delighted to see his friends. And his funny little monkey Mischief jumped up to hug Timmy, and then got on his back — the animals were the best of friends too!

'Isn't this a stroke of luck?' cried Tinker. 'We'll all be on the same cruise together! What fun we're going to have!'

The children stayed in the garden for some time, making all sorts of plans. Professor Hayling was working in his laboratory and didn't want to be disturbed — not even for the children to say hallo to him.

Then Jenny, the Haylings' housekeeper, came

out of the house. 'Come along in!' she told the children with a big smile. 'I've made you a nice tea!'

Plump, bustling little Jenny was almost like a mother to Tinker, who had lost his real mother when he was very small. When she saw the Five arriving out of her kitchen window, she had set to work to make them feel at home. She knew they had good appetites, so she had baked a big chocolate cake, and made one plate of tomato sandwiches and another of sandwiches oozing with honey! There was home-made lemonade to drink.

The children thanked her, and sat happily down at the tea table. Soon they were all chattering away as they ate their tea. After telling each other about last term at their different schools, they turned to a subject which was in the news a lot at the moment.

'I say, did you hear the radio news at lunch-time?' Tinker asked his friends. 'Apparently the Black Mask is in the headlines again!'

'The Black Mask?' asked Anne, puzzled. 'What's that? I've never heard of it.'

'He's not an it – I mean, it's a he!' said Julian. 'He's a famous international jewel thief – he isn't part of a gang, he operates on his own. Well, I dare say the police will soon catch up with him, Tinker.'

Julian was a very sensible, level-headed boy, and never let himself get carried away – unlike his cousin George! 'Oh, I don't agree, Julian!' she cried now. 'I think the Black Mask is too cunning to let himself be captured so easily. He seems to be as clever as a bagful of monkeys – oh, Mischief, don't pull my sleeve like that, I wasn't talking about *you*! And as he hasn't got any accomplices he doesn't have to worry about someone giving him away, which can happen in a gang. Working on his own protects his anonymity.'

'His what?' asked Anne, who didn't know the long word.

'I mean, no one knows who he really is.'

'Not even the police?' asked Anne, surprised.

'Of course not, fathead!' replied Dick. 'If they did he'd have been behind bars long ago, wouldn't he?'

'So long as there was some evidence against him to put him there!' said George, smiling. 'I say, wouldn't it be fun if *we* tracked him down? I bet we could, too! He wouldn't suspect us of being after him because we're so young – but we're brave and dynamic and intelligent –'

'And terribly modest!' laughed Tinker. 'Well, George, if you want to spend your holidays chasing the Black Mask you'll have to give up the idea of our cruise! You won't be meeting *him* on board the *North Wind*! He must be far too busy stealing jewels to take a holiday like that.'

They were all getting interested in the exploits of the famous, mysterious thief known only as the Black Mask, and went on talking about him for a while.

'He only steals very valuable things,' Dick told his sister Anne. 'I mean, he steals jewels and so on from rich women. And it said on the radio that he's recently broken into the strongroom of a bank in Buenos Aires. That must have been pretty difficult – I wonder how he did it?'

'We can read the details in the newspaper, I expect,' said Tinker. 'But the Black Mask isn't just a thief, he's a spy too!'

'A spy?' said George, who hadn't known about that.

'Yes – my father says he's stolen all sorts of secret documents from scientists and diplomats of different lands. Then he sells them to whatever country's government will offer the highest price.'

'I wonder why I've never heard of him before?' asked Anne.

'Because your head's always in the clouds,' Dick teased her. 'And there aren't any jewels up in the clouds for the Black Mask to steal!'

Anne shivered a little at the thought of the crimes committed by the famous jewel thief who was also a daring spy. She had a sweet nature, and hated the idea of violence or dishonesty, but she had keen eyes too, and her gift for observation was often a great help to her cousin and her brothers when they were in a tight place. People found Anne very disarming, with her pretty face and her kind heart.

Tinker looked at his watch.

'Five-thirty,' he said. 'Let's go and watch the

early evening news on television. Perhaps there'll be some more about the Black Mask.'

He took his friends into the sitting room and switched on the television set. Sure enough, the newsreader was just talking about the international thief's latest exploit.

'Once again, a visiting card bearing the picture of a small black wolf was found in each of the safes the Black Mask had forced. The thief uses these cards as a way of putting his signature to his crimes, and it demoralises his unfortunate victims. Mr da Silva, the manager of the robbed Argentinian bank, was in such despair, feeling he had betrayed the trust placed in him, that he thought of committing suicide.'

'How dreadful!' said George indignantly. 'That poor man! Why, the Black Mask is worse than a thief – he's as bad as a murderer!'

'I quite agree,' said Julian.

'And to think that he's still on the loose!' said Dick. 'Only the other day he was in Monaco, stealing the takings from the casino there, then he went to Buenos Aires – where will he turn up next?'

'Well, never mind!' said Tinker. 'He's nothing to do with us! Let's forget about him and think of the lovely holiday we're going to have!'

Chapter Two

IN THE HOTEL

Next day all was bustle and excitement at Kirrin Cottage! George, her parents and her cousins were getting ready to leave. They set off by train the following day, and reached Southampton late in the afternoon.

The organisers of the *North Wind*'s cruise had booked rooms in an hotel for all their passengers. They were to spend that night on land and go on board the liner next morning.

The Kirrins and Haylings had come on the same train, and after washing their faces and tidying up, George, Julian, Dick, Anne and Tinker came down to the hotel lounge to wait for supper-time – or rather, dinner-time, because they would be having grand grown-up evening dinner on this exciting holiday!

Poor Mischief, who hadn't enjoyed the train

journey much, was complaining, with his arms firmly wrapped round Timmy's neck as if he were asking the dog to look after him. Kind Timmy licked him now and then in a comforting way. The two animals made a funny, touching couple, and were soon attracting a lot of interest from the hotel guests waiting for dinner to be served.

'How amusing!' said a dark man wearing glasses, who had a slight foreign accent. 'I never saw anything so funny!'

Tinker smiled at the foreigner, who smiled back and patted first Timmy and then Mischief. The man wore a signet ring with a huge, glowing ruby in it on the fourth finger of his hand.

Then the children heard a shrill, complaining voice. 'Those animals ought not to be allowed in the hotel! I'm *sure* they've got fleas!'

George cast an angry glance at the speaker – what an insult to her beloved Timmy! She was an old woman who looked as vinegary as she had sounded, and with her hooked nose and sharp chin she looked like everyone's idea of an old witch in a fairy-tale.

'My dog has *not* got fleas!' said George loudly.

'Nor has my monkey!' agreed Tinker in an indignant voice, letting everyone know!

A cheerful fat man with a red face burst out laughing. 'Don't you children take any notice of that lady,' he whispered, pointing to the 'witch'. He seemed to be foreign too, though he spoke

17

excellent English. 'I've been sitting next to her for the last hour, and she does nothing but grumble about anything and everything. She just *likes* to find fault!'

George, who was rather quick-tempered, wasn't mollified by that. '*Horrible* old woman!' she muttered through her teeth.

The old lady heard her, and gave her a very nasty look!

A slim Chinese girl had been watching the little scene in silence. She smiled in a way that might have been either mocking or sympathetic – it was hard to tell which from her face.

'Well, come along!' said a distinguished-looking gentleman, abruptly getting up from his chair. He had very long, white hands. 'I believe they're serving dinner now.'

He seemed to want to relax the atmosphere in the hotel lounge. Strolling across the room, he went into the dining room, followed by the rest of the hotel guests, except for the Five and Tinker, who were left alone waiting for Uncle Quentin and Aunt Fanny to come downstairs.

'Well!' said George angrily. 'If that old witch is going to come on the *North Wind* with us, I'd rather stay behind on land with Timmy!'

'In that case, young man,' said a voice behind her, 'you'd better resign yourself to staying on land!'

George jumped. A man of about thirty was

'Those animals ought not to be allowed in the hotel.'

'Let me tell you about a few more of our travelling companions.'

getting up from an armchair. He had been hidden from the children's view by the back of his chair.

'What do you mean?' George asked.

The stranger smiled. 'I'll explain, young fellow.' Like so many people, he obviously thought George was a boy! 'I know a little about most of the people you've just met, and a number of them *are* coming on the cruise. There's the foreigner with the ruby ring – his name is Pedro Ruiz, and he's known almost all over the world. He's a rich Brazilian coffee planter. The cross old lady is called Mrs Ivy Flower – she may have a pretty name, but she's seen three husbands into their graves already!'

The children smiled.

'She's immensely rich, and thinks that gives her the right to say whatever she likes about everything!'

'Well, my dog would have shown her she was wrong if I'd just given him the word to attack her!' said George confidently.

'He may yet get the chance! As you guessed, Mrs Flower is one of the *North Wind*'s passengers.'

'Are *you* going to be on the cruise too?' asked Julian.

'Yes – my name's Ben Moore. But let me tell you about a few more of our travelling companions! The jolly, fat man is a Dutch diamond merchant called Mr Van Dam. The distinguished-looking gentleman with the beautiful hands is the famous pianist Francis Barraclough. And the Chinese lady is called Miss Ping.'

Julian introduced himself and the others. Ben
Moore shook hands with all of them, and smiled at
George. 'I'm so sorry – I really thought you were a
boy!' he said. But George didn't seem to mind!

In the dining room a little later, the Five and
Tinker took the opportunity of studying their
companions for the cruise – or those of them Ben
Moore had pointed out. Mr Moore himself, who
was sitting at a table near the children, gave them a
friendly wink now and then.

'He's nice, isn't he?' said Dick.

'Nicer than Mrs Flower, anyway!' muttered
George, patting Timmy under the table.

'Oh, well!' said Julian philosophically. 'I suppose a cruise is a bit like life – you're bound to meet
all sorts of people! Some nice, some not so nice –'

'And some perfectly horrible!' George finished,
in her forthright way. She still bore Mrs Flower a
grudge for being so rude about her dog.

'George, you oughtn't to talk like that!' said
Julian. 'If Uncle Quentin hears you –'

'Don't worry, Julian,' said Tinker. 'The old
dears aren't nearly close enough to hear!' And he
pointed irreverently at George's parents and
Professor Hayling, who were indeed sitting at a
table some way off, deep in what seemed to be a
fascinating discussion.

'What a good thing there wasn't a table big
enough for all of us! If you ask me, it's much nicer

being on our own without any grown-ups!'

'Oh, Tinker!' said Anne gently. 'You don't mean that! Your father and Uncle Quentin and Aunt Fanny are so kind, and they let us do nearly everything we want!'

'Yes, and doing things on our own is part of the fun,' said Tinker cheerfully. 'Well, let's hope they don't interfere while we're all together on the ship – though if I know your father and mine, George, when they get together they can't think of anything but their scientific work!'

*　　*　　*

Next day everyone was up early, eager to go on board the *North Wind*. Several coaches came to drive the passengers to the quayside. George exclaimed in delight at her first sight of the white ship with its elegant lines, which was going to be their floating home for the next few weeks.

'Isn't the *North Wind* a lovely ship?' she cried. 'She looks like a big seagull perching on the water, ready to fly far, far away!'

George loved the sea! Dick grinned at his cousin. 'Well, we always knew you were brave and intelligent and straightforward and so forth, but I never knew you were a poet too, Georgina dear!'

George, who hated being called by her full name, put out her tongue at him. Then she said, in her usual cheerful way, 'Quick, let's go on board! I want to explore the ship!'

Stewards were putting luggage in the cabins, and the passengers were moving in, making a lot of noise. Then most people went up on deck to see the ship leave Southampton.

Slowly, the beautiful white liner left the quay. The sun was shining brightly and the sea was a clear blue. They couldn't have had a better start for the cruise.

Leaning on the rail, Julian, Dick, Anne, George and Tinker watched the white foam of the waves breaking against the ship's side. The *North Wind* moved on slowly and gently, as if giving her passengers time to enjoy the feeling that they were under way at last.

'This is wonderful!' said Anne. 'The air seems twice as good out here!'

'Let's go and get our bathing suits,' suggested George. 'There's a swimming pool on deck. We can bathe, and then lie in the sun and get brown!'

The children were about to go down to their cabins when they heard several people behind them, talking excitedly.

Some of the passengers had just settled in comfortable loungers on the deck to read that morning's newspapers – they had bought the papers just before they came on board. And it was obviously something they were reading which was making them all exclaim out loud.

'Have you seen this article?' asked one old

gentleman. 'It must be a practical joke – but it's very alarming! Such things oughtn't to be allowed!'

'Maybe someone just wants to ruin this cruise for us?' suggested a young woman.

'Oh, I don't think so!' quavered an old lady. 'I'm taking it seriously. Why – we might all be murdered in our beds! It's shocking – dreadful!'

'Don't upset yourself, Miss Brown,' said another woman, who had just finished reading the article they were all discussing. 'The Black Mask certainly is a notorious criminal, but he's not a murderer! Even if he was really on board the *North Wind*, it wouldn't be to kill anyone!'

The children looked at each other in surprise.

'The Black Mask – on board this ship?' said George. 'What luck! Suppose we managed to *un*mask him! We'd be even more famous than we were before!'

'Modest little shrinking violet, aren't you, George?' Tinker teased her.

'We must find out just what's in this newspaper story which seems to be getting them all so excited,' said Dick. 'Oh, I wish *we* had a copy of the paper!'

And in a trice his wish was granted! Timmy, with Mischief sitting on his back and urging him on, went straight over to a deck chair where someone had left a newspaper. The naughty little monkey picked up the paper and offered it to Tinker in triumph. Tinker was very surprised!

'Did you ever see anything like it?' he asked the others. '*I* think Mischief and Timmy understand every word we say! They're more intelligent than most human beings.'

'Let's see the paper,' said George. And almost tearing the newspaper out of her friend's hands, she impatiently opened it.

'Listen!' she exclaimed. 'THE BLACK MASK GOES ON A CRUISE – that's the headline! And the writer of the article goes on like this – "By the first post this morning, the editorial offices of all the daily papers received one of the Black Mask's familiar visiting cards with the picture of a black wolf." '

The four others gathered round George, listening intently as she read aloud. ' "The famous international criminal's cards also bore the words, 'With the compliments of the Black Mask, who would like you to know that he is taking a holiday on board the cruise liner *North Wind*.' " Well, what do you make of that?' George said, folding up the paper again.

'What cheek!' cried Julian. 'If the Black Mask really wrote that message he must be mad! Why – he'd be giving the police a good chance to lay hands on him at last.'

'It must be a hoax of some kind,' said Tinker.

'But suppose it really *is* true?' Anne ventured to suggest.

They heard several of the other passengers still

talking indignantly.

'Why did they allow this cruise to take place, with a threat like that hanging over our heads?'

'It's madness!'

'We must ask the Captain for an explanation!' someone cried.

But before anyone had time to move, a voice from a loudspeaker asked for silence. It *was* the Captain speaking! Captain Parker said he had an announcement to make. He had heard about the passengers' worries and he wanted to reassure them. The *North Wind*, he said, had not put to sea until the police had made a quick but thorough search, and the Black Mask was definitely not on board. The identities of all the passengers were known, and none of them had any criminal record. The staff were above suspicion too. The papers had been over-hasty in publishing the story, and the authorities had asked the BBC not to broadcast it over the radio for fear of alarming the public unnecessarily. It was just a practical joke in very bad taste!

'And in any case,' the Captain finished, in a cheering tone, 'remember that even if by some extraordinary chance the Black Mask really *was* here among us, the mere fact that he's said so would prevent him from committing any crime. He would very soon be found and arrested! A boat is like a little floating island with a strictly limited number of inhabitants! And now, the crew and I would like to wish you a very happy cruise on board the *North Wind*!'

Soft music from the loudspeaker took over from the Captain's voice. George was looking so downcast that Dick couldn't help laughing.

'You'll just have to resign yourself to it, old thing! We must make the best of a bad job – no Black Mask on board for our amusement! What a shame!'

Julian, Anne and Tinker began to laugh too, Timmy barked, Mischief uttered happy little squeals, and George finished up by laughing at herself. And so they forgot about the Black Mask – for the time being, that is!

Chapter Three

SOME MAGIC TRICKS

The first few days at sea passed very pleasantly. The *North Wind* was to sail straight down past the coasts of France and Spain, and through the Straits of Gibraltar, going on to pick up some more passengers at the port of Marseilles. After that the real, sight-seeing part of the mystery cruise would begin. But it was fun just being on the boat those first few days! Passing the Rock of Gibraltar was a great thrill for the children – most of the time, however, they were very happy with all the open-air amusements the ship had to offer. They could swim in the pool, and play all sorts of deck games. They explored every bit of the liner where passengers were allowed, making all kinds of interesting discoveries. Soon they knew their way all round the upper and lower decks and all the gangways. There wasn't any first and second class on board this cruise liner, just one class for everybody, which made it easier to look round besides being friendlier.

On the day they reached Marseilles, the children went on shore to look round while the other passengers came on board. All the passengers met in the dining room that evening, and they had good appetites from the sea air! After dinner the Five, Tinker and Mischief went up on deck.

'I'm a bit tired – we've seen so much today!' said Anne, yawning. 'I'm sure I shall sleep well tonight!'

'You're not going to bed yet, are you?' protested Dick. 'We're allowed to stay up later than usual while we're on this cruise – why don't we go and watch the film they're showing in the shipboard cinema?'

'No – let's go and watch the conjurer,' said Tinker. 'The purser told me he's going to give a show tonight and it'll be very good.'

'Oh, yes!' Anne agreed eagerly. 'I'd love that!'

'Honestly, Anne!' said George rather scornfully. 'Conjuring tricks are just for babies who can't see how they're done!'

'Well, let's go and see the show, all the same!' Tinker insisted. 'It'll make a relaxing end to a nice day!'

And he dragged the others off to the dining room. The tables had been cleared, and some of the stewards were busily transforming it into a little theatre.

'What's the conjurer's name?' asked Julian.

'I don't know,' Tinker said. 'But the purser said how good the show would be – he explained that they'd engaged a conjurer to entertain the passengers on this trip, and though he wasn't very well known yet they thought he was excellent!'

The children were lucky enough to get seats in the very front row. Like the good dog he was, Timmy lay down at George's feet – and Mischief fell asleep leaning against Tinker's shoulder!

Suddenly an elegant-looking man walked out on the stage which had been set up facing the audience. He was smiling. He wore evening dress and a top hat, and he was holding the conjurer's traditional 'magic wand'.

'Goodness me!' said George, suddenly getting interested. 'It's our friend Ben Moore!'

'I noticed that he never told us what *he* was doing on the *North Wind*!' said Julian. 'So he's the ship's conjurer! That must be an amusing job to have. Oh, he's seen us!'

Julian was right. Ben Moore had spotted his young friends in the audience, and he gave them a little private nod of greeting.

Then he launched into a whole stream of funny patter, and began his tricks. Anne watched open-mouthed as he juggled with some white balls which disappeared into thin air one by one. Then he turned a canary into a baby rabbit, and swallowed a string of sausages which unexpectedly turned up inside his top hat! In fact, he was performing all the usual sort of conjuring tricks people expect to see.

There was a short interval, and then Ben Moore did some different tricks – tricks of his own invention this time, or so he said. The audience watched in amazement as he turned a little jet of water into a firework! He had some funny props too – one of them was a little car with square wheels, but when he got in it the wheels went round perfectly all right! Next came the high point of the show. Ben Moore asked for a volunteer to be 'beheaded'. Dick went up on stage. 'It's all done with mirrors!' he whispered to Anne, who was looking rather worried.

Ben Moore moved his hands about a bit – and there was Dick's head apparently suspended on its own in space, while the boy went on talking to the conjurer. Dick didn't seem to have noticed anything at all himself!

There was loud applause for this trick.

'Hurray!' shouted George. 'Jolly good!'

'Did you enjoy my magic tricks?' Ben asked, leaning forward to speak to the audience.

'Oh yes, we loved them!' replied Mischief, suddenly waking up.

Before Tinker had got over his surprise at hearing his monkey talk, *Timmy* spoke up! 'Well, I never did! I never heard a monkey talk before!'

George was absolutely baffled for a fraction of a second, and then she burst out laughing. She had

There was Dick's head apparently suspended on its own in space.

'Oh yes, we loved them!' replied Mischief.

just realised it wasn't really the animals who were talking! Ben Moore was a ventriloquist as well as a conjurer.

Everyone clapped hard when the show was over. The children went over to the stage to congratulate Ben Moore before going back to their cabins. They liked Ben a lot, and felt glad he was a friend of theirs.

George was sharing a cabin with Anne – and with Timmy too, of course. The three boys were in a cabin next to the girls. The boys' cabin had four bunks, so they had plenty of room.

They all slept soundly that night, and met again at breakfast next morning. Uncle Quentin and Professor Hayling were already deep in discussion over the breakfast table, talking about the fascinating work they were doing.

Aunt Fanny said she would leave the children to do as they liked that day. Now that the mystery cruise had really begun, the passengers were told, Mr Daley the purser would let them know where they were going each day in the morning. They would never know their destination more than a couple of days in advance! When he appeared in the dining room everyone stopped talking.

'Today we sail along the coasts of France and Spain,' said Mr Daley, smiling. 'We shall pass several ports, and drop anchor for the night off the Spanish port of Valencia. Tomorrow morning we head for the Balearic Islands, where we shall visit Ibiza!'

There was a happy murmur of anticipation as he went out again.

'So they're only going to tell us where we're bound for bit by bit!' said Dick.

'I think that's a good idea, don't you?' said Ben Moore, joining the children. 'It makes a change from the sort of cruise where everything feels almost *too* well organised, all drawn up to a strict timetable. With luck I'll have some time to relax on this trip!'

Then he kindly offered to show the children round Valencia after dinner that evening. They were very pleased, because when the time came Aunt Fanny had a headache, and didn't feel like going on shore. As for Uncle Quentin and Professor Hayling, they had been working on a very interesting problem all day, and said they didn't want to 'waste their time' sight-seeing!

So everyone was delighted with Ben's suggestion. The conjurer said he had been in Spain before, and knew the country quite well. He and the children were about to start out when Miss Ping, the pretty and rather mysterious Chinese girl, asked if she could come with them.

'You sound as if you know your way round Valencia,' she said to Ben. 'I'd be so pleased if I could go with you too.'

Before Ben had time to reply a tall, strongly-built young man with a lot of thick hair came over to them, smiled, and asked, 'May I join the party as

34

well? My employer's gone to bed – he told me to go on shore and amuse myself, but it's not much fun going on my own.'

The young man had a nice, cheerful face. The children knew who he was: his name was Luke Martin, and they had seen him pushing his employer John Bayley's invalid chair. Mr Bayley was a businessman who had broken his hip in a car accident last winter, and still couldn't get about except on crutches. He preferred to stay in a wheelchair while he was on board the *North Wind*. Luke was travelling with him as his nurse and secretary.

The children would really rather have gone on their own with Ben Moore, but they couldn't say no to Miss Ping and Luke Martin without seeming rude!

Anyway, Ben was already giving the other two passengers a welcoming smile, and saying, 'Yes, by all means do join us, both of you! But it's too late to go visiting monuments and museums today. 'We'll have to make do with seeing something of the night life of Valencia – like all Spanish towns, it's a lively, jolly place at night.'

So Ben led his party round the brightly lit streets. He was right – the children thought Valencia was as busy as if it had been broad daylight. Everyone seemed to be out and about!

'That's the Spanish custom,' the conjurer explained. 'People have what they call a siesta –

that means a rest on their beds in the afternoon, the hottest time of day – and then they all go out in the evening.'

When they had seen enough, he took his party into a busy side-street and ordered refreshments for them all on a café terrace.

The children felt very grateful to Ben for giving them such a fine outing, and told him so. Ben winked. 'Tomorrow we'll be seeing Ibiza – in daylight this time,' he said. 'It's a beautiful island. You're sure to like it!'

They soon reached the *North Wind* again. It was a warm night, and the air seemed almost scented. The children, Miss Ping and Luke Martin thanked Ben, and they all went to their own cabins.

'What do you think of Miss Ping, George?' Anne asked when they were alone. 'I like her!'

'She's a bit like a panther – a gentle one,' said George. 'Or a cat with its claws drawn in, making velvet paddy-paws! You can't be sure just what her smile might be hiding.'

'What about Luke Martin? I think *he's* nice too – he's so amusing!'

'Mmm ... yes ... well, good night, Anne!' murmured George. 'I'm terribly tired.'

Next morning, Mr Daley the purser told the passengers that after their visit to Ibiza the *North Wind* would be stopping at a place called Isola Rossa on the island of Corsica. 'We'll spend the day there,' he said, 'so you'll have plenty of time to take

36

photographs and bathe in the sea if you like.'

The visit to Ibiza was great fun. Nearly all the passengers went on shore. They seemed very cheerful. Those of them who had been afraid the Black Mask might strike were beginning to feel reassured. No one had heard any more about the adventurous jewel thief, and there was no sign at all that he was on board the liner.

'You see, there wasn't anything to worry about,' Dick told Anne. 'The Black Mask isn't on board.'

'I'm not so sure,' said the little girl. She suddenly looked very thoughtful. 'Ben bought an English newspaper in Valencia, and that didn't say anything about the Black Mask either! Perhaps he's just not committing any crimes at the moment – or perhaps he *is* here with us after all!'

'Well, if he is, he won't be stealing anything from us!' someone said behind Anne. 'Don't you remember what the Captain said? If the Black Mask went stealing valuables on board a ship he'd be giving himself away – it would be easy to find him among such a small number of people!'

The speaker was Francis Barraclough the pianist. Anne thanked him, with a shy smile. She was always ready to like people, and she thought the famous musician was a very kind man to take the trouble to soothe her fears.

'Oh, Mr Barraclough, I do hope you're right,' she said gratefully.

The little groups of passengers were really

enjoying themselves on the beautiful island, with its flower-covered slopes standing above the blue sea. Everyone said how lovely it was – except for Mrs Ivy Flower, of course! *She* complained of everything – the sun, the wind, the rocky ground, and even poor Timmy, though he was keeping well away from her. He knew by instinct that she didn't like him!

On the way back, however, Miss Ping, who was walking just behind the children and Aunt Fanny, suddenly let out a little cry.

'Oh, my brooch!' she said. 'It's gone!'

Chapter Four

THE FANCY DRESS BALL

'That brooch has great sentimental value for me!' cried Miss Ping. 'It belonged to my mother.'

They immediately stopped and searched for it, retracing their steps. They looked at the sparse hedges and every tuft of grass, and even inspected the pebbly path, but the brooch did not turn up.

Poor Miss Ping was very upset. George and her cousins and Tinker could remember just what the lost brooch looked like. It was made of gold, very prettily engraved, set with a star-shape of diamonds – a real work of art!

At last they had to resign themselves to going back to the ship empty-handed. The brooch had disappeared without trace. Mrs Ivy Flower made things even worse. 'I don't think you *lost* your brooch,' she told the Chinese girl. 'Mark my words, it was stolen! And who stole it? Why, the Black

Mask, of course! That fellow is capable of anything!'

'Oh yes, of course!' agreed Mr Van Dam the fat Dutchman, laughing. 'To be sure, it was that terrible Black Mask did it! Why, *I* lost a couple of pounds yesterday evening, playing cards – but of course I didn't really lose them, the Black Mask stole them! Ha, ha, ha!'

Mrs Flower was furious. She obviously didn't like people to make fun of her. She tightened her lips and didn't say another word. Well, that was *one* good thing!

Later that afternoon, the *North Wind* anchored off Isola Rossa on the Corsican coast.

'Oh, Julian, do get your camera!' said Dick. 'You'll be able to take some splendid photographs here!'

Like everyone else, George was admiring the sight of all the little islets dotted about in the sea. But she seemed to have something else on her mind too – and she had! Somehow, she couldn't rid herself of the idea of Miss Ping's brooch having been stolen by the Black Mask. She wondered if, just for once, Mrs Flower and her suspicious nature might be right.

'Perhaps the Black Mask really did steal that piece of jewellery?' she said to herself.

She didn't let her cousins and Tinker know what she was thinking, though. She was afraid they would laugh at her – they were always telling her she was over-imaginative.

'And they may be right!' she sighed. 'It certainly does seem rather a far-fetched idea. I mean, the Captain assured us none of the passengers had any criminal record! Now that I'm coming to know our companions on this cruise *I* don't see any of them in the part of the Black Mask either. So I'd better try to think about something else!'

Nothing unusual happened next day, which they spent ashore. After lunch the children sunbathed on the beach. And when the passengers went back on board the *North Wind* to change for dinner, there was a surprise waiting for them.

The purser announced that there would be a dance that very evening. 'A fancy dress ball!' he said. 'We want everyone – grown ups as well as the young people – to dress up, using whatever they have here on board, as imaginatively as possible. There will be prizes!'

George and her cousins were delighted. What fun – an improvised fancy dress ball! They chattered about their ideas for costumes all through the meal.

'I know what *I'm* going as!' said Julian. 'All I need is a sheet, and I'll make a very fine ghost.'

'I'm going to dress up in a sheet too,' said Dick. 'But mine will be a Roman toga! I'll wear my sandals too, and try to brush by hair into curls, and go as Julius Caesar.'

'Wasn't he bald?' said George, laughing. 'I'm

41

going to dress up as a pirate!'

'And I'll be an organ grinder, with my monkey!' said Tinker, his eyes twinkling. 'I'm sure I can find an old cardboard carton in the kitchens, to make myself a barrel organ.'

'I'm going to be Queen Cleopatra!' said Anne. 'I'll use my striped towel to make an Egyptian head-dress.'

'And I shall come as an Indian snake-charmer!' said Ben Moore, who was sitting with his young friends. 'It doesn't seem quite fair on other people, but I have some very good costumes with me for my job!'

The other passengers were making their plans too. George glanced at Mrs Ivy Flower. '*She* could dress up as a witch, or the Bad Fairy!' she muttered. 'All she needs is a broomstick!'

At nine o'clock the band began to play a cheerful tune, and one by one the passengers who had said they would be coming to the fancy dress ball appeared. Aunt Fanny happened to have brought a gauzy trouser suit with her, and she was dressed up as an Eastern dancing girl – but Uncle Quentin and Professor Hayling stayed in the smoking room. No fancy dress balls for them!

Mrs Flower made everyone smile. She had dressed up to suit her name, and was covered with artificial flowers! Goodness knew where she had found them, and she looked very odd, but for once she was smiling.

Mr Van Dam came wearing a red skull cap, with his cheeks painted vermilion. He was a Dutch cheese, and being so fat and round he made a very good one too!

Suddenly, everyone stiffened. A man in black evening dress, with his face hidden by a black mask, had appeared in the doorway of the saloon. The Black Mask! Miss Ping, who was looking lovely in a genuine Chinese robe, uttered a cry of alarm. And then they all breathed again in relief. It was only Mr Stone, a thin, rather silent man, who always wore dark glasses – though not a black mask! – in the daytime.

The passengers' surprise turned to amusement when a second 'Black Mask' made his appearance. This time it was Pedro Ruiz, the rich Brazilian. And there was loud laughter when a third Black Mask followed him – Francis Barraclough. Everyone was in fits of merriment when a *fourth* Black Mask turned up, in the shape of Luke Martin!

'Well, well!' said Mr Stone ruefully. 'That should teach us to be more imaginative! And I thought I'd make quite a sensation with my original idea!'

The fancy dress ball was a great success. George and her cousins and Tinker had a lovely time all evening. When it was time for the prizes to be given, John Bayley, the invalid, turned up in his wheelchair. He couldn't dance, but he wanted a look at the fun.

The passengers' surprise turned to amusement when a second 'Black Mask' made his appearance.

Mr Daley the purser awarded first prize to – Mrs Ivy Flower! The old lady smiled broadly. Privately, the children thought Mr Daley probably wanted to soften her up and improve her temper!

'Now, more music!' said the purser. 'The ball goes on till midnight!'

But before the band could start playing again, a large woman ran up to the purser. She was very upset.

'Oh, Mr Daley! This is dreadful! My diamond necklace has been stolen. Stolen from my neck while I was dancing with my husband!'

It was Mrs Herrington, one of the richest women in America! Her husband, who owned a great many oil wells, didn't seem nearly so upset.

'Never mind, dear,' he said coolly. 'Your jewellery's insured. The insurance company will pay up!'

'But meanwhile I've lost my necklace – and it means that thief is on board after all!' his wife exclaimed.

'Maybe you simply mislaid it?' suggested the purser. 'Or it dropped off?'

'No, that's impossible. It has a double safety catch. Someone would have had to undo it – and anybody who managed to do *that* while I was actually wearing it must be very clever indeed!'

Then George let out a little cry.

'Oh! Just look what I've found on the floor!'

And she handed Mr Daley a little card with the

picture of a small black wolf in the top left-hand corner.

'It's one of the Black Mask's visiting cards!' cried the purser, horrified.

'And there's something scribbled on it in pencil!' Dick pointed out, craning his neck to see.

'So there is!' said Julian, reading it. 'Listen – "With the compliments of the Black Mask, and many thanks to Mrs Herrington for her very handsome donation!" '

Chapter Five

WHERE IS THE NECKLACE?

A deathly hush fell. Mrs Ivy Flower was the first to break it.

'I said so all along! The Black Mask *is* here on board the *North Wind*! He could be any one of us!'

George could hardly keep from clapping her hands! She was delighted to think that she and her cousins had the chance of solving yet another fascinating mystery. Dick looked at her.

'I say, George, you look pleased! *You* rather thought the Black Mask was on board too, didn't you?'

Anne didn't say anything. She was very willing to help her brothers and her cousin, but she didn't go looking for adventures herself. She was too gentle-natured and sensible for that.

Julian seemed rather serious. Tinker dug an elbow into his ribs. 'What's the matter, Julian?' he

47

asked. 'This is a real gift for us!'

'You bet it is!' said George. 'What a chance to spice this exciting holiday up with a bit of *extra* adventure!'

'Woof!' said Timmy approvingly.

'Teehee!' tittered Mischief, not to be left out.

'Please, don't be alarmed,' Mr Daley was saying calmly. 'I must report this to the Captain at once. Would you all kindly stay here until I come back?'

As he went out, all the passengers present began looking suspiciously at one another. They were all telling themselves that the Black Mask *was* there among them, and might be the very person sitting next to them at that moment.

'Well,' said Julian, 'the fact that not all the passengers came to the fancy dress ball will make it easier for the Captain and the shipboard detective to carry out their inquiries.'

'My father and Professor Hayling weren't here,' George remarked, 'so *they* won't be bothered.'

'And we're too young for anyone to suspect *us*,' said Tinker, rather relieved.

'And Aunt Fanny is a woman,' said Anne.

'So she is!' said George solemnly. 'But have you thought that the Black Mask might just as well be a woman as a man? After all, no one knows the thief's real identity!'

Dick laughed. 'My money's on Miss Ping!' he said. 'She looks so mysterious sometimes.'

'I wish it could be Mrs Ivy Flower!' said George.

'Then she'd be shut up in the hold, and poor old Timmy could stop trembling so hard at the sight of her! He's such a brave dog, but he's really frightened of Mrs Flower.'

'Woof!' afreed Timmy, with deep feeling.

'Do stop being so silly,' said Julian. 'Here comes Mr Daley with the Captain.'

Captain Parker was accompanied by a thin, dark man. He introduced him to the waiting passengers.

'This is Mr Vernon, a private detective employed by the company who owns this liner. He's going to make some preliminary inquiries straight away, and I'd be glad if you would all help him as much as you possibly can. Thank you very much.'

One by one the passengers went up to the table where the detective was sitting. They all gave their names and then made statements, including George and her cousins. George showed the detective where she had found the Black Mask's visiting card, but that was all she could tell him. At last, all the passengers present were searched, and then they were allowed to go back to their cabins. The necklace had not been found!

The next day was a very busy one for Mr Vernon the shipboard detective. With the help of the ship's officers, he searched all the passengers' cabins. No one dreamed of objecting.

'They're quite right to do it,' Mr Stone said. 'When nothing is found in our luggage, that will prove us innocent.'

'This is Mr. Vernon, a private detective.'

George showed the detective where she had found the Black Mask's visiting card.

Nothing was found in *anyone's* luggage! The four cousins and Tinker met by the swimming pool later that day. It was deserted – even the keenest swimmers seemed to have other things to think about.

'The Captain is very upset,' said Julian. 'Mrs Herrington's necklace hasn't come to light, and the Black Mask is on board this ship after all, but no one can identify him – so I suppose we have the threat of more thefts hanging over us!'

'I heard it wasn't just the cabins that were searched, but the whole ship,' said Anne.

'Yes, that's right,' replied Tinker. 'Captain Parker and Mr Vernon think the Black Mask may have hidden the necklace not in his cabin, but somewhere else – in some place where he thinks he can recover it later.'

'I suppose all the luggage will be searched again when the passengers leave the *North Wind* at the end of the cruise?'

'Yes, of course, Anne,' said George. 'But people can't be prevented from going on land *during* the cruise – and it would be difficult to search them every single time! So the Black Mask may be able to seize his chance to go ashore and send the necklace to his own address by post.'

'Well then,' said Dick, 'all we have to do is watch everyone when we go ashore – anyone seen making for a post office is a suspect! Maybe we'll manage to discover the thief that way.'

George sighed. She wasn't very hopeful. 'There are only four of us to follow people – five counting Tinker,' she said. 'We're easily outnumbered by the passengers who came to the fancy dress ball. We can never hope to shadow all of them!'

'Perhaps Uncle Quentin and Aunt Fanny would help?' suggested Anne. 'And Professor Hayling?'

Tinker, who was sitting on the edge of the swimming pool swinging his legs, was so surprised he almost fell in!

'Don't be silly, Anne!' he said. 'I mean, can you *see* my father and your Uncle Quentin interrupting their boring old discussions for anything at all? They couldn't care less what goes on round them – all they're interested in is their work. I bet they don't even know a necklace has been stolen! I wouldn't like to be sure they even remember they're on a cruise at all!'

'You're exaggerating a bit, but you're not so far wrong, Tinker!' said George smiling. 'Anyway, I'm afraid my parents wouldn't approve of us doing detective work in case it becomes dangerous.'

'Dangerous?' asked Anne in alarm. 'How do you mean?'

'Well, the Black Mask won't be very pleased with us if we do find out who he is, will he?'

'Anne shivered. 'You're right,' she said. 'We'd be taking quite a risk!'

But that didn't worry brave little George! She was very excited to know that the Black Mask really was on board, and she fully intended to do her best first to identify him, then to get him arrested! However, it was certainly a risky undertaking, and they'd have to be both careful and clever. But the Five, Tinker and Mischief made a strong team. George knew that if they all co-operated they could work wonders. And as they were only children – and a good dog and a sweet little monkey – the Black Mask would never suspect them of being after him, or dream that *they* were making inquiries, as well as the shipboard authorities. Perhaps they might have a better chance than Mr Vernon, the official ship's detective!

Chapter Six

ANOTHER ROBBERY

The *North Wind* had spent an extra day lying at anchor off Corsica, so that Captain Parker could get in touch with the police, and Mrs Herrington could report her loss to the insurance company. Then the liner set off southwards down the western coast of the island.

It was still wonderful weather, and gradually the atmosphere on board relaxed. The Corsican police at Isola Rossa had searched the ship themselves – the cabins, the luggage and the passengers – and thorough as they had been, nothing had turned up! Once the first alarm was over, the passengers recovered their spirits. After all, they had come on this cruise to have a good time, and most of them were determined not to let the mysterious Black Mask spoil it. They thought there was no reason why he should strike again.

Mr Daley was trying to make sure they all enjoyed themselves. They went on shore to visit some picturesque creeks near a place called Piana, and take photographs. The passengers taking part in this excursion set off in small groups along the coastal road, which had reddish cliffs falling away to the sea on one side of it.

'No point keeping a watch on anyone here!' Dick whispered to his cousin George. 'There's no post office anywhere in sight.'

'Let's keep our eyes open, all the same,' George said in the same low tone. 'You never know what may happen!'

The five children thought the scenery was very beautiful. Even Timmy seemed impressed by the magnificent view from the top of the coastal road. There was a parapet to keep people from falling over the cliffs, and Timmy put his paws up on it and stayed there for quite a long time, barking hard.

George, who was watching Julian take some photographs, got rather annoyed with him and told him to be quiet. Timmy looked crestfallen and came back to her. Anne was posing for her photograph, with her fair hair blowing in the breeze. Dick and Tinker were a little way off, laughing at Mischief, who was delivering what seemed to be a long speech to a little donkey which had suddenly come out of the undergrowth and stopped right in the middle of the road, staring at the surprising sight of the monkey!

When everyone had taken all the photographs they wanted, Mr Daley, who had come on shore with Ben Moore to act as guides to the party, said they were now going to have lunch at a café in Piana.

They climbed down to the village in good spirits. The donkey seemed to have made friends with Mischief, who ended up by jumping on his back! So the donkey joined the party too. Seeing a baker's shop, George popped in to buy some bread and fed him – dear old Timmy did look as if he were a little jealous!

They were all pleased to reach the café and sit down. And they were in the middle of a very good meal, when Mrs Ivy Flower's shrill voice suddenly interrupted the rest of the conversation.

'Why is there another place laid beside mine? It bothers me – why doesn't someone take it away?'

Mr Daley signed to a waiter and said something to him in a low voice. The waiter seemed surprised. He took a list out of his pocket and consulted it.

'But, sir, you said there would be eighteen guests in all, didn't you?'

'Yes,' said the purser. 'Yes, there are eighteen people on this excursion. The other passengers said they would rather stay on board. But why do you ask?'

'There are only seventeen of you, sir! That place you asked me to take away was laid for the eighteenth. One of your ladies or gentlemen can't

56

have arrived yet, sir!'

The purser quickly counted the people present. Yes, the waiter was quite right – there *were* only seventeen people having lunch.

George, who had been listening to the whole conversation, counted too. The group who had come ashore to see Piana included all the passengers who were really keen on seeing the sights everywhere they went. That meant the five children – Julian, George, Dick, Anne and Tinker – with their friend Ben Moore, Miss Ping, Mrs Ivy Flower, the Brazilian planter Pedro Ruiz, Mr Stone, Francis Barraclough the pianist, Mr Van Dam the Dutch diamond merchant, John Bayley, who liked to join in when he could and had Luke Martin to push him in his chair, Mr and Mrs Herrington and Aunt Fanny. Then there was the purser himself, of course. That made eighteen – and there were only seventeen people at the table!

'It's Mr Ruiz who isn't here!' George said. 'But I *did* see him, not long before we arrived. He was standing a little way away from us, taking photographs!'

Everyone looked round as if that might make the missing Mr Ruiz magically reappear.

'Yes,' said Ben slowly. 'You're right, Mr Ruiz isn't with us. Where on earth can he be?'

'You say you saw him on the road going along the cliff-tops?' the purser said, turning to George.

'Woof!' said Timmy.

57

'Yes, I did,' replied George. 'But I didn't take any special notice of him. I wish I had, now!'

Only her cousins and Tinker realised how cross George must be feeling with herself. After telling the others they must keep their eyes open, *she* had been distracted by the beautiful scenery. And now Pedro Ruiz had disappeared! George was furious with herself.

'He can't be very far off,' said Mr Van Dam optimistically.

'Perhaps he's just wandered off for a moment,' said Mr Stone.

'But he hasn't been here at lunch – and he'd have had plenty of time to rejoin us!' said the purser, obviously worried. He rose from the table. 'Stay here and enjoy the rest of your meal,' he told the others. 'I'm going to look for Mr Ruiz.'

'I'll come with you!' suggested Ben on impulse.

'Can we come too?' George and Julian asked at the same time.

'Why not?' said Ben. 'Young folk like to be active, don't they? Come along, then!'

All the Five got up from the table, and so did Tinker, with Mischief perched on his shoulder. After making sure that the Brazilian wasn't anywhere in the café itself, the little party set off along the cliff-top road. They saw no sign of Pedro Ruiz. He might have vanished into thin air!

'I just can't understand it,' muttered the purser.

He was interrupted by an urgent 'Woof!' from

Timmy. The dog had run to the parapet overlooking the sea and was barking as hard as he could. Then he turned to look eloquently at George.

'My dog's seen something!' she cried. 'He was barking at something on this very spot earlier, too. Let's go and have a look!'

She hurried off without waiting for anyone else. The others followed. Timmy was still barking. Head stretched out, he seemed to be looking at something lower down the cliff. George leaned forward – and saw a human form lying on a rocky ledge between two bushes. The waves of the sea were breaking down below.

'Oh, my goodness!' cried Anne, leaning over the parapet too. 'It's poor Mr Ruiz! I can tell because he always wears such bright clothes – that's his purple suit with the pink stripes!'

'Yes, it *is* him!' said the purser grimly. 'We must get him up, fast!'

'Look – he's tied up,' said Ben, who had good sharp eyes. 'Well, I must say!'

'Come on, there's no time to lose!' Mr Daley said to him. 'The two of us should be able to get him up here.'

George and Dick clambered over the parapet after the two men, though Julian protested and Anne begged them not to. Neither of them minded heights! And that was just as well, considering the steep drop to the sea from the narrow ledge where

59

'Oh my goodness! It's poor Mr Ruiz!'

the Brazilian planter was lying.

The four rescuers got down to the unconscious man easily enough. Pedro Ruiz had his eyes closed. A wound just above his right temple seemed to show that his attacker had hit him before tying him up.

With some difficulty, Mr Daley, Ben, George and Dick hoisted the Brazilian up to the parapet, and Julian, Tinker and Anne helped them get him over.

They put the poor man down in the shade on a grassy bank. Ben cut the thin cord binding his hands and feet with a pocket knife, and rubbed his wrists and ankles to get the circulation going. Anne gently moistened his temples with some eau de cologne which she had with her.

In a moment or so Pedro Ruiz came back to his senses. 'Where am I?' he asked.

Then, before anyone could tell him, his memory seemed to come back. His eyes flashed angrily.

'Where's that villain who attacked me?' he shouted. His loud voice told the others that he wasn't feeling *too* ill. 'Oh, if I can only get my hands on him he'll be sorry!'

'Who was it?' asked Mr Daley eagerly.

'How should I know?' grunted Pedro Ruiz, feeling his head. 'I'd gone off to get some better photographs of those interesting rocks, and I was a little way from the rest of the party, when someone suddenly grabbed me from behind. I think it was a judo grip. My head struck the ground, quite hard – and that's all I remember!'

'My dog saw you down there on a rocky ledge,' began George, 'and then –'

But she was interrupted by Mr Ruiz saying something very angry in Portuguese! He was seething with rage. 'Look at this!' he cried – in English this time. 'I've been robbed – look! My pockets are empty, my wallet's gone, everything! Even the valuable ruby ring I was wearing. Ah – what's this?'

Frantically going through his pockets, he had just found a small card with the picture of a black wolf on it.

George recognised it at a glance. 'The Black Mask again!' she cried. 'So *he* was in our party today! What a nerve he's got!' And she added in a low voice, speaking to her cousins, 'Good! This will make things much easier for us!'

Never mind poor Pedro Ruiz and his troubles – George was delighted! The Black Mask's latest crime would surely lead to his downfall! She felt that the Five would soon discover who he was, now that the suspects were narrowed down to today's shore-going party.

Chapter Seven

HOW MANY SUSPECTS?

On board the *North Wind* that evening, everyone was talking about the attack on poor Mr Ruiz. Another search had been made, with no results. The Black Mask had had plenty of time to hide his loot. Mrs Ivy Flower was making all kinds of alarming prophecies.

'You just wait and see, we'll all be murdered in our beds one by one!' she said. 'And *then* don't say I didn't warn you!'

She seemed to be rather enjoying this sinister idea – not that anyone was really listening to her.

After dinner George, Julian, Dick, Anne and Tinker went on to the upper deck with Timmy and Mischief. They had found a place there in the shelter of one of the lifeboats, where they could talk in peace.

'What are we going to do now?' Julian asked

George. 'Mrs Herrington's necklace has been stolen, and Mr Ruiz's wallet and ring – possibly Miss Ping's brooch, too! And we've hardly got anywhere with our investigations yet!'

'We'd better do some hard thinking,' said George. 'It's a good idea to have a well thought-out plan before we go into action.'

'Right!' said Dick. 'For a start, let's see what suspects we've got!'

'Yes, let's!' said Tinker. He was very glad to be sharing in one of the Five's adventures again! 'Why don't we make a list of all the people who went on the excursion today, and eliminate anyone who can't possibly be under suspicion? Then we'll know the Black Mask must be one of the others!'

'Did you notice that all the people who were with us today were at the fancy dress ball too?' said Anne.

Julian took a piece of paper out of his pocket, and began writing down the names of the passengers who had gone on the expedition to Piana. Then he read them out loud to the others.

'Yes, that makes eighteen,' said George. 'And there are several names we can cross off the list straight away!'

'Beginning with Aunt Fanny and ourselves!' said Dick. 'That makes six suspects less!'

'Don't forget Mr Daley the purser and our friend Ben,' added Anne.

'Right – eight!'

'We can cross poor Pedro Ruiz off too,' said Julian. 'And Mrs Flower. She's so thin and frail, I can't see *her* using a judo grip on Mr Ruiz!'

George interrupted him. 'Steady on! We mustn't judge by appearances! Pedro Ruiz might have faked that attack – he could easily have given himself a slight wound on the forehead and put a bit of cord round his own ankles, and even his wrists. After that, all he'd have had to do would be to *say* the Black Mask had robbed him.'

'But what for?' asked Tinker, puzzled.

'To draw suspicion away from himself if he *does* happen to be the Black Mask! As for Mrs Flower, she may be stronger than she looks, and there's no reason why she shouldn't know judo. After all, it's *meant* to be a way for weak people to defend themselves against stronger ones – or to attack them!'

'All right, we'll leave Ruiz and your dear friend Mrs Flower on the list, if you like,' Julian agreed. 'But we can cross Mr Bayley off. He's an invalid.'

'*Is* he? How do we know for sure?' asked George.

The others looked at her open-mouthed.

'We think he's an invalid,' George went on, 'because he says he is, and he seems to have difficulty getting about. But if he's really the Black Mask his illness could be faked, just as cover.'

Dick nodded. 'You may be right. If so, Luke Martin must be his accomplice. Well – what about Mr and Mrs Herrington?'

'Like Ruiz, they could easily just be pretending to be victims of the Black Mask's thefts.'

'Well then,' said Dick, 'that leaves us with ten suspects: Mr Stone, Mr Van Dam, Francis Barraclough, Mrs Ivy Flower, Miss Ping, Mr and Mrs Herrington, Pedro Ruiz, John Bayley and Luke Martin!'

'That's right.'

'Quite a lot of people!' said Tinker.

'Mr Barraclough is far too nice to be a criminal!' Anne protested.

'Now, Anne – in detective stories it's always the person who seems most innocent who turns out to be guilty!' Julian reminded her.

'Why not ask Ben to help us?' suggested Dick. 'I've already told him about some of our adventures, and he seemed very interested.'

'Yes, I'm sure he'd take us seriously,' said George. 'All the same, I'd rather we kept it to ourselves.'

'I don't agree,' said Julian. 'The Black Mask is a dangerous criminal. Having a grown-up on our side could be useful – and Ben is a good sort!'

George still objected, but finally she gave way, and the Five and Tinker went off to find Ben. When they told the young man all about it, he promised to help them.

'I'm flattered to be asked!' he said. 'I'm entirely at your disposal – but don't forget you're dealing with a resolute and very clever man. Unmasking him won't be easy!'

The *North Wind* spent the night in the Bay of Ajaccio, and next morning the passengers visited the town before the ship put to sea again – making for Algiers! This was very exciting! The children had never guessed that their cruise would take them as far as Africa, and they were thrilled.

None of the passengers seemed to be thinking of interrupting their trip and leaving the *North Wind*. Those of them the Black Mask had already robbed thought they had nothing more to fear from him – and the rest intended to get their money's worth out of the trip! If the Black Mask was offering them a challenge, they were going to take it up.

'And of course,' George pointed out, 'anyone who left the ship now might be suspected of *being* the Black Mask! At any rate, the police would be sure to ask a lot of questions. So no one wants to make a fuss.'

'And the Herringtons and Mr Ruiz know their insurance companies will pay up!' added Ben, laughing.

All the passengers were in the dining room for breakfast next day. Captain Parker invited the children to sit at his own table. Julian, Dick, George, Anne and Tinker were very pleased, and took the opportunity of asking him some questions about the 'Mystery of the Black Mask', as some of the passengers were calling it.

The Captain's face clouded over.

'That wretched fellow is ruining our cruise,' he said. 'Mr Vernon's keeping his eyes open the whole time – he just hopes he'll soon find out who the thief is!'

Drops of sweat stood out on the poor man's forehead as he thought of all the responsibility he had to bear. He pulled his handkerchief out of his pocket to mop the sweat away – and out came a little card too! It fell on the floor. Quickly, George bent to pick it up. Then she froze in astonishment.

She was holding one of the Black Mask's visiting cards!

The children looked at the Captain in astonishment. Captain Parker! Could *he* be the famous criminal? No, surely not – and yet, there was the card!

Before they had got over their surprise, Mischief suddenly jumped up, looking cross, and snatched the card away from George. Then, chattering to himself, he ran to put it back in the Captain's jacket pocket, where it had been just a moment before.

Tinker burst out laughing. He realised what had happened!

'I apologise for my monkey, Captain! He's such a naughty little thing – he was playing a trick on you!'

Several of the passengers who had seen the incident were looking at the visiting card. Captain Parker had taken it out of his pocket again.

'But that's mine!' Pedro Ruiz suddenly cried.

'That is, it's the same card the Black Mask left on *me* yesterday after he attacked me! I recognise it! Look – here's a tiny drop of blood from my wound, in the right-hand corner. I left the card in my cabin, and –'

'And Mischief must have stolen it from you and put it in my pocket!' finished the Captain with a faint smile. 'Good heavens, what a fright that little monkey gave me!'

Everybody laughed!

Leaning on the ship's rail, George watched the coast of Africa go by. What an exciting holiday this was! They arrived in Algiers that afternoon, and spent several hours visiting the town.

Next day, the really keen sight-seers – and even some of the other passengers – got into a hired coach to go and visit some very interesting gorges. Of course George and her cousins and Tinker had found themselves seats near the front of the coach, and Timmy and Mischief were there too.

'The place we're visiting today is very picturesque,' Mr Daley the purser told the tourists. 'The famous "Monkeys' Stream" flows through the gorges. As you can guess from its name, tribes of monkeys live near this stream.'

Dick thumped Tinker on the back. 'I hope you'll keep Mischief on a leash, old chap! We don't want him running away.'

'Don't worry,' said Tinker. 'He's too fond of me to go off with other monkeys!'

69

The gorges were certainly very beautiful, and the children were impressed by the sight of the tall trees growing there. The monkeys chattering all around them made a lot of noise. Mischief tugged at his leash – not because he wanted to join the other monkeys, but because he'd seen a little Arab boy with a cart, selling peanuts!

Then Timmy was attacked by two monkeys who pulled his tail and ears – and Mischief, forgetting about the peanuts, bravely came to his defence, boxing the other monkey's ears. The tourists, attracted by the strange sight, gathered round the animals, laughing.

Suddenly they heard a cry! George and the others swung round. Miss Ping was facing a big monkey standing in her path, a little way from the rest of the party. Suddenly the animal picked up a stick and raised its arm, as if it were about to attack the young woman.

Before anyone could help her, a surprising thing happened. Slender Miss Ping, far from seeming frightened, marched straight up to her attacker, seized the hairy arm threatening her, turned round and flung the big monkey over her head, not letting go of his arm. He landed on the ground, uttering cries of terror! Then she let go of him. In one bound, the animal got up and fled. He could be seen disappearing among the trees – he didn't want any more! The children exchanged meaning glances.

'Did you see that?' whispered Anne. 'Miss Ping

Miss Ping flung the big monkey over her head.

'Did you see that?' whispered Anne. 'Miss Ping knows judo!'

knows judo! And wasn't she cool and collected?'

'Yes,' agreed Dick in a whisper. 'Who'd have thought it? Miss Ping looks like being our Suspect Number One!'

'Yes,' said Julian thoughtfully. 'She certainly *could* have attacked Pedro Ruiz!'

As the Five went back to Algiers in the coach, they were promising themselves to keep a particularly close watch on Miss Ping. Ben agreed that that would be a good idea. Now he knew she was a judo expert, he said, *he* suspected the slender Chinese girl might be their quarry, too!

Chapter Eight

THE BLACK MASK STRIKES AGAIN

After a lovely cruise along the coasts of Algeria and Tunisia, the next stop was to see Carthage! The *North Wind* anchored in the Gulf of Tunis, at the very foot of the ancient city. Magnificent white houses set among palm trees rose to the Cathedral of St Louis.

'Queen Dido founded the famous city of Carthage in the year 878 BC,' Ben told his young friends.

George, her cousins and Tinker were very glad to have Ben as a guide again! He seemed to have travelled widely and seen everything!

This time, almost all the passengers wanted to go ashore to see the famous ruins.

'Listen,' George told the others. 'All we have to worry about is our ten suspects. They're the only ones who have always been somewhere near by when the Black Mask stole something – so that eliminates everyone else.'

'I'm sticking close to Miss Ping,' said Tinker.

'And the rest of us will manage to watch the other nine!' said George confidently. 'We'll be everywhere at once!'

'Come off it, George!' smiled Julian. 'Nobody can be in two places at once!'

'I think I'll keep an eye on Mrs Flower for you,' said Ben. 'She's already asked me to take her round Carthage, so it's quite convenient.'

'Well, I hope you have a nice time!' said Dick cheerfully.

It was a very hot day. Francis Barraclough the pianist, who said he was feeling rather tired, sat down on a stone in the shade of a ruined temple gateway to rest. The children could see him from some way off. He was on his own, smoking a cigarette.

And then, a little later, when they were all on their way back to their coaches, Mr Barraclough suddenly cried, 'My watch! I've lost my watch!'

It was a platinum watch, he explained, and very valuable!

'The last time I looked at it I was over there – by the entrance of that old temple!' he said.

'Oh, yes!' said George. 'You stayed there for quite a long time, didn't you? Perhaps it just dropped off your wrist – let's go and look!'

She ran towards the ruined gateway, followed by

the others. They soon found the place where the pianist had sat down to rest – but there was no sign of his watch. Instead, very easy to spot, they saw a small white card jammed between two stones.

Another of the Black Mask's visiting cards!

'Oh no!' cried George, really furious. 'Just fancy stealing Mr Barraclough's watch under our very noses! He's laughing at us!'

'That means we can cross Mr Barraclough off our list, doesn't it?' said Anne.

'No, it doesn't,' Dick told her. 'He's still a suspect, just like the other two of the Black Mask's victims – or so-called victims!'

'Let's ask him if anyone came by while he was resting here,' said George.

But the musician said he hadn't seen anyone except Mrs Flower, with Ben escorting her – and the old lady had only exchanged a couple of words with him. Then he cried, 'Oh, wait, there *was* someone else! I saw Mr Bayley and Mr Martin – they stopped beside me for a moment, but I really can't suspect either of *them*!'

George thought fast. Mr Barraclough was inclined to be absent-minded, and she was afraid he could easily have talked to other people too and forgotten *that*!

The tourists had been spread over such a wide area that the Five had had difficulty trailing their nine suspects without losing sight of them – especially as they didn't want to be noticed doing it.

Tinker was the only one who felt he could be quite sure. He said he'd stuck so close to Miss Ping that he could swear *she* wasn't guilty after all.

'In fact she got quite annoyed in the end, and asked me not to keep following her about like that!' he told his friends. 'So then I didn't follow quite so closely – but all the same, I never lost sight of her. We can cross her off the list of suspects!'

Meanwhile the coach drivers were asking the passengers to get back on board, and the children hurried in.

There was a short drive from Carthage to an Arab village where they were to stop to admire the landscape and drink mint tea. On the way, Julian took the list of suspects out of his pocket and quietly crossed off Miss Ping's name.

'I never really suspected her myself,' he told George in a whisper. 'Somehow I can't see a woman as the Black Mask.'

'Well, I still think Mrs Flower may be a suspect! I'm going to keep with her when we reach this village. Ben tells me he had to leave her after about quarter of an hour, because she was getting on his nerves so much, complaining of everything. So we don't know what she did after that. Well, now *I'll* be her guide and support her tottering footsteps!'

True to her word, when they reached the Arab village George went up to Mrs Flower and offered to keep her company.

Mrs Flower glanced at her suspiciously. 'Hmph! Very well, if you want,' she said at last.

George *didn't* want – quite the opposite! But she told herself that if the Black Mask were to strike again on this excursion, then at least they'd know where they were so far as the old lady was concerned! The passengers from the *North Wind* were getting very tired of all the thefts and attacks that were taking place whenever the liner stopped. They were wasting so much time making statements to the police that it was really getting on their nerves.

After drinking mint tea in a café the tourists went off to explore. George went with Mrs Flower, as they had agreed. Timmy ran ahead of them, wagging his tail as if to show how glad he was to be one of the party!

George had to be very patient! Her companion insisted on leaning on her shoulder as they climbed a very steep stairway leading to a viewing point. Poor George was soon out of breath, but she stuck to her task. At last the old lady seemed to be satisfied. She said she had seen enough, and she was going back to the coaches now.

When they came in sight of their coach, George and Mrs Flower saw that their travelling companions seemed to be upset about something. They were talking excitedly and waving their arms about. Dick saw his cousin and waved to her. She came running up.

'George, Mr Van Dam has been attacked!' Dick told her.

'That's right,' said Anne. 'He wasn't with the

others, poor man! Someone jumped on him and grabbed the jacket he was carrying over his arm. Mr Van Dam didn't get a chance to recognise his attacker, but the man was wearing a black mask – and a costume like the one Mr Stone wore to the fancy dress ball. He ran away very fast. Mr Van Dam is rather fat, so he couldn't catch up. He found his jacket on the ground a few minutes later.'

'But his wallet had gone,' finished Julian. 'And what do you think he found instead? One of the Black Mask's visiting cards!'

'I insist on being searched!' Mr Stone was shouting indignantly. 'If I'm the thief, then no doubt I shall have the wallet on me! I demand to be searched – I *insist* on it!'

'I'm not accusing you!' said the fat Dutchman, crossly. 'Let's go and make a statement to the local police!'

Of course nothing came of that. Mr Stone had not got Mr Van Dam's wallet on him, and Mr Van Dam had to resign himself to losing his money. Mr Vernon, the shipboard detective, was obviously feeling very cross. The Black Mask had escaped him yet again!

'In any case,' murmured George thoughtfully, as their coach drove along the road to Tunis, 'now I can cross dear Mrs Ivy Flower off the list!'

'We only have eight suspects left!' said Dick.

'Seven men and a woman,' added Tinker.

'Have you noticed how *often* the Black Mask is

striking at the moment?' asked Anne. 'As if he were trying to defy everyone – Mr Vernon, the Captain, the other passengers, the police, and even us!'

'I wonder what will happen in Tunis?' said George. 'At this rate I have an idea it'll be something else unpleasant!'

Ben Moore chuckled. He realised that George wasn't really very pleased to find that Mrs Flower, who disliked Timmy so much, couldn't be suspected! Timmy himself looked downcast. His mistress's glum mood had infected him, and though Mischief made faces to amuse him it was no good.

Tunis was only a few miles from the village they had visited, so the tourists soon got there. They were to have a real Tunisian meal at the Africa Hotel.

The Africa Hotel stood in the middle of the town, near the Grand Mosque. It was a very modern six-storey building, with four lifts, and there was a lot of coming and going. The hotel lounges were on the fifth floor and the dining room on the second floor.

Most of the tourists, who felt thirsty, went straight out on the terrace to enjoy a nice cool drink. Others preferred to rest in the lounges, and some of them wanted to walk round the huge reception area, where there were glass cases full of things to buy, and a fountain of water to keep the place nice and cool.

The children thought it would be fun to sit at the bar on high stools, while most of the grown-ups

The barman uttered a cry of alarm.
'The red light! Help! Thieves.'

chose more comfortable chairs. Drinking delicious iced orange juice, the five friends discussed the day's events.

'Mr Stone is my favourite suspect now,' said Tinker. Naughty Mischief was stealing from a dish of olives!

'We must be fair and keep our minds open,' said Anne. 'The Black Mask may *look* a little bit like Mr Stone, but that's no real reason for us to suspect him.'

'Have you noticed that this is the first time anyone's actually *seen* the Black Mask?' said Dick.

'Yes,' replied George, gloomily. 'Mr Van Dam said he was quite tall and thin, so it's a man – unless it was Mrs Herrington, who's wearing a trouser suit today!'

'Anyway, that lets Mr Van Dam himself out of it,' said Tinker. 'He's short and fat!'

'That *would* let Mr Van Dam out of it,' George sighed, 'if only we could be sure he's telling the truth. But how do we know he really was robbed? We only have his own word for it. And he was the only one to see the Black Mask – so he may have made up that description of him!'

'That's true,' said Julian.

'In other words,' concluded Dick, 'we're going round in circles!'

'Yes – unless –'

But George broke off as the barman uttered a cry of alarm.

'The red light!' he cried. He pointed with a trembling hand to a light winking on and off on the wall beside him.

'What does it mean?' asked Dick.

'It's an alarm signal from the manager's office!' stammered the barman. 'Bells should be ringing all over the hotel – but I suppose the wires have been cut! Mr Haziz the mangager must have managed to press the button which works that signal. It's a hold-up! Help! Thieves!'

Chapter Nine

A HOTEL RAID AND A SHIPBOARD CHASE

The barman was shouting at the top of his voice, and at the same time he set off another alarm bell which was worked from the floor of the hotel they were on. In a moment the whole place was a hive of activity! The staff were all running about, and the hotel guests, who had no idea what was going on, were asking questions and not getting any replies.

'The police!' cried George. 'Someone must telephone the police at once!'

That was certainly the first thing to do. But even before the police arrived, they found out what had really happened. Mr Vernon, Mr Daley, Ben, the Five and Tinker all met, and they got someone to show them where the manager's private office was. They ran off there, followed by the hotel receptionist.

The door of the room was wide open, and they

found Mr Haziz, the manager, lying unconscious on the carpet. Anne and George hovered round the poor man while Mr Vernon called a doctor.

Soon the manager came to his senses and explained that he had been counting the day's takings, when someone burst through the door and hit him. Mr Haziz had just had time to switch on the red light before losing consciousness, thanks to a button hidden under his desk.

Of course the safe had been emptied! There was nothing in it now but one of the Black Mask's visiting cards – proof enough that he had committed the crime!

When the police arrived at last, Mr Haziz described his attacker. He said the man was wearing an Arab robe, but he seemed to be quite tall and thin – and he had a black mask over his face.

George took her cousins and Tinker aside, looking gloomier than ever.

'The Black Mask isn't making things very easy for us,' she sighed. '*Any* of our suspects could have put an Arab robe on over their ordinary clothes and whisked it off again in a trice!'

'The man who held up the manager was tall and thin,' Julian reminded her. 'That bears out what Mr Van Dam said. So now we *can* be certain Mr Van Dam himself isn't the Black Mask!'

Tinker looked hopeful.

'Yes, that's one good thing!' he said. 'The

number of suspects is down to seven now!'

* * *

Next day the passengers from the *North Wind* were to visit the markets of Tunis. Julian, Dick, Anne and Tinker really enjoyed going round the steep alleyways where the merchants put their picturesque wares out for sale. At one point Mischief escaped Tinker and shut himself inside a big wicker birdcage shaped like a mosque! The passers-by laughed. But George was still glum. She was thinking that in spite of all the risks the Black Mask took, no one had come anywhere near tracking him down yet. Not the police, not Mr Vernon – not even the Five themselves!

'We've done our best, I know,' she thought. 'But we can only work by a process of elimination – and that's not what I call *real* detective work!'

She was forgetting that Mr Vernon knew even less than she did! But she really took as a personal insult the casual way the Black Mask was boldly outwitting everyone in the course of this cruise.

The *North Wind* put to sea again, making for the Gulf of Qabes. They anchored there late in the afternoon and spent the evening on board. Though everyone now knew the international jewel thief was among them, the passengers had made up their minds to enjoy themselves as much as they could. The air was wonderfully fragrant, and music played while they ate dinner. Directly after the meal, the five children went up on deck with Timmy and Mischief to sit in the starlight and discuss the fascinating subject of the Black Mask.

'The suspects still on the list,' said Julian, producing it, 'are Mr Ruiz, Mr Stone, Mr Barraclough, Mr Bayley, Mr Martin, and Mr and Mrs Herrington.'

Anne sighed. She was tired.

'After so much activity on land I expect the Black Mask, whoever he is, will want to cut down on the risks he's taking and get a bit of rest now! I know *I* do – I'm sleepy. Coming to bed, George?'

'What, now?' said George indignantly. 'It's far too early for bed!'

'Let's go and find Ben,' suggested Julian. 'I believe he's rehearsing some new tricks for his conjuring show tomorrow – perhaps he'll let us watch.'

'Good idea!' cried Dick, jumping up from his chair. 'Come on!'

'We really ought to be keeping watch on our suspects,' said George. 'Pedro Ruiz and Mr Van Dam are playing chess in the smoking room. That'll keep *them* busy for some time! But the other six –'

'Well, Mr and Mrs Herrington are in the saloon talking to Aunt Fanny,' Anne said.

'In that case,' said Julian, 'we're left with Mr Stone, Mr Bayley and Mr Martin, and Francis

Barraclough. But I agree with Anne. I don't think the Black Mask will try anything this evening. Let's go and see Ben!'

George hesitated. 'All right,' she said at last. 'But we won't stay with him long – afterwards we must try to find out just how our suspects are spending their time this evening!'

The children went down from the deck and started for Ben's cabin, which was some way off. The thick carpet in the gangways muffled their footsteps. Suddenly, turning a corner, Tinker, who was in front, stopped short in surprise.

'My word!' he whispered to the others. 'There's someone trying to get into Mr Van Dam's cabin!'

The five children stood perfectly still. In the dim light of the gangway, they saw a man bending over the lock of the Dutchman's cabin door, obviously busy picking it!

The children looked hard at the man. He seemed to be rather tall and thin, and he wore a dark suit. To her delight, George saw that he was wearing a black mask too! She signed to the others to tell them to creep up without making any noise, and then all jump on the Black Mask together!

But Mischief ruined her plan. He let out a frantic chattering. The man turned his head. His eyes, shining through the holes of the mask, saw the children, and he reacted at once. Swinging round, he ran for the far end of the gangway, and they all chased after him!

'There's someone trying to get into Mr. Van Dam's cabin!' Tinker whispered.

It was a desperate race!

It was a desperate race! George and Dick led the way, with Julian after them. Then came Tinker and Anne. Urged on by his little mistress, Timmy turned the corner before anyone else.

'The Black Mask can't escape us now!' gasped George. 'Timmy will get him!'

But before they reached the end of the gangway they came to another passage crossing it, and two more passages led off *that*. Which was the one to take?

'Timmy!' called George.

A bark from her right was the answer, and they all turned that way – only to run straight into Ben, who was coming towards them, with Timmy happily running beside him.

'Oh, blow,' said Dick crossly. 'What's happened?'

'That's just what I'd like to know!' said Ben, intrigued. 'What's going on? You should just see your own faces!'

George quickly explained that they had been close on the heels of the Black Mask. Ben uttered an exclamation of annoyance.

'So *that* was it! What a fool I am! I've ruined it all. I was just coming out of my cabin when I saw old Timmy here shoot past like an arrow. I didn't think I might be spoiling anything – I just called to him and he stopped and came to me. I thought he must be chasing the ship's cat!'

'Well, it's too late to make up for lost time now,'

sighed Julian, disappointed. 'The Black Mask will have had plenty of opportunity to hide.'

'We can still try,' suggested Ben. He obviously wanted to make up for his mistake. 'You go that way, I'll go this way, and perhaps we'll find a clue.'

But the Five, Tinker and Ben explored that part of the ship in vain.

'Are you sure it was Mr Van Dam's cabin the Black Mask was breaking into?' Ben asked the children. 'You are? Let's go and look!'

Sure enough, there were recently made marks on the lock, showing that someone had tried to force it.

'We must tell the Captain and Mr Vernon, and Mr Van Dam too,' decided Julian.

Mr Van Dam was still in the smoking room playing a game of chess with Pedro Ruiz. He said he and his opponent hadn't moved from there all evening, even for a minute! So one more thing was clear now – Pedro Ruiz could be crossed off the list of suspects too.

Then George had an idea. She went to the saloon to see if her mother and the Herringtons were still there – it certainly looked as if *they* hadn't moved either! But to make sure, George signalled to her mother from the doorway. Aunt Fanny excused herself to the Herringtons and went over to George.

'Yes, George dear, what is it?'

'Mother,' said George, 'someone tried to burgle Mr Van Dam's cabin just now. Have Mr and Mrs Herrington left you at any time in the last hour?'

'No, not even for a second,' said Aunt Fanny.

'We've been in here talking ever since dinner.'

'Good – thank you very much!'

And George hurried off to join the others. 'The American couple are in the clear too,' she told them.

'How many people do you still suspect?' asked Ben.

'There are only four left,' said Julian, looking at his list, which was full of crossings-out now. 'Francis Barraclough, Mr Stone, Mr Bayley and Luke Martin.'

'That's splendid!' cried Ben cheerfully. 'The advantage is all on our side now! There are only four of them – and six of us to watch them, even without counting Mr Vernon – or Timmy, of course!' he added hastily, for fear of hurting George's feelings.

But George didn't seem as enthusiastic as she might have been. She was less talkative than usual, too.

Dick couldn't help teasing her a bit, when Ben had left them. 'Well, old thing, what's wrong? Your nose seems to have been put out of joint!'

'You know quite well what's wrong!' said George huffily. 'I feel as if the Black Mask were just laughing at us. He's striking more and more often now, as if he felt sure he could get away with anything. It was only luck that we foiled his attempt at burglary this evening – and even so he got away!'

Actually George was a little ashamed of the way

she was feeling. She had a generous nature – and yet somehow she grudged having Ben let into their secret and helping them.

'Tinker is one thing,' she said to herself. 'He's an old friend – though if Mischief hadn't made that noise I'm sure we'd have caught the Black Mask! But Ben is different – he's a perfect stranger, and it isn't as if he was really being much *help*! I mean, he called to Timmy and took his mind off his job – and I bet our enquiries would be going twice as fast if we were working on them alone!'

Yes, George was ashamed of her private thoughts. It wasn't a bit like her to think such things – and yet somehow she couldn't help it.

Of course Mr Vernon's latest inquiries got nowhere. However, as the Black Mask's attempt at burglary had been unsuccessful, and most of the passengers didn't even know about it, everyone was in a good mood when they went on shore next morning.

Chapter Ten

THE WHITE GLOVE

They were going to visit an oasis. It was a lovely place – there were red pomegranate flowers among the green leaves, and a spring of water fell into a stone basin. Little Arab boys dived to pick up the coins thrown to them by the amused tourists.

As they all crowded round the spring to get a better look at this picturesque scene, one of the passengers – a young woman whom George and the others didn't know very well – suddenly cried, 'Help! Thief! My handbag!'

The children looked round. They saw a thin man wearing an Arab robe, running away.

'The Black Mask!' cried George at once. 'Quick, everyone! We won't let him escape this time. Come on, Timmy – good dog! Catch him!'

As Timmy was taking off, Mischief jumped on his back and clung to his neck, urging him on with

Timmy had already got the thief on the ground, while Mischief pulled his hair.

'It's not the Black Mask after all.'

shrill little cries – but Timmy needed no encouragement!

In a few bounds, he had caught up with the thief. The man dropped the handbag he was holding, to try to defend himself. But Timmy had already got him on the ground, while Mischief, knocking off the man's head-dress, pulled his hair.

The thief howled, letting out a flood of Arabic words.

'Gosh – the Black Mask is going in for local colour all right!' said Dick, running along beside George. 'Talking Arabic! I didn't know he was good at languages too!'

Followed by some of the other tourists, they soon caught up with the thief and Timmy. George told her dog to keep the thief just where he was. The man lay there motionless, face downwards.

'Right – now get up!' said George triumphantly. 'Take your mask off and let's see your face!'

It was an exciting moment. The man got up and turned round – and everyone could see he wasn't wearing the famous black mask! He was a brown-faced Arab, and he looked both terrified and furious at having been caught.

'Oh no!' cried Julian. 'It's not the Black Mask after all!'

No – they had only caught a petty local sneak-thief! George was disappointed, but she had to make the best of it. The Five *still* couldn't boast of having caught the famous, elusive Black Mask.

95

The *North Wind* was gently riding the waves, still anchored in the Gulf of Qabes. The heat was so fierce that afternoon that most of the passengers took a siesta. Aunt Fanny, Uncle Quentin and Professor Hayling had gone to lie down on their bunks. Ben had gone to his own cabin. The children were a little bored, left to their own devices.

'We could play Scrabble,' said Anne, who liked quiet games.

'All right, if you like,' agreed George. 'I'll go and get the Scrabble board. See you in the saloon!'

She hurried off, followed by Timmy. The gangway seemed dark after the blazing sun outside. But then she suddenly saw a patch of white some way ahead of her – a white-coated steward was just coming out of Mr Van Dam's cabin.

Loud snores came from the Dutchman's bunk – Mr Van Dam was asleep. George smiled. The steward quietly closed the door after him and then hurried off.

Suddenly George's smile vanished! In a flash, she understood the meaning of the little scene she had just witnessed. It looked so ordinary – but it *wasn't*! That steward had no business in Mr Van Dam's cabin, because if Mr Van Dam was asleep he couldn't have rung for a steward!

'Hi!' called George, hurrying after the man. 'Hi – steward!'

But the steward didn't stop and turn to face her! He began to run – and disappeared from sight.

'Stop thief!' cried George, without pausing to think. 'Stop thief! It's the Black Mask!'

She felt instinctively that she wasn't wrong this time! There was a lot of noise around her, and then loud exclamations as cabin doors banged open and shut. George and Timmy turned the corner of the gangway and saw their quarry at the other end of the passage.

'Get him, Timmy!' cried George.

And then she regretted raising the alarm – because the passengers who had been roused by her shouts thronged out into the narrow gangway. They got in her way – and more important, Timmy's! There were even *more* people in the next gangway. Quite a little crowd had gathered – with two or three stewards among them. George realised she had been foiled again.

However, Timmy came back to her in triumph holding a white glove in his mouth!

'So the Black Mask is wearing gloves!' George told herself. 'In order not to leave fingerprints, I expect!'

'What is it? What's happened?' voices all round her were asking.

She didn't have to reply – loud shouts were suddenly heard from Mr Van Dam's cabin. She ran back there, and found the diamond merchant gesticulating wildly.

'I've been robbed! My superb collection of diamonds and rubies – it's gone! And to think I refused to put it in the ship's safe, thinking it would be better to keep it with me! I had the stones inside a canvas belt which I wear next to my skin night and day – but it was so hot today I took the belt off, just for my siesta. And the Black Mask has seized his opportunity to steal it! Look – here's his card!'

When Mr Vernon the detective was told, he could only confirm that the jewels certainly *had* disappeared. George offered him the white glove Timmy had found.

'It may be a clue – and may not be!' muttered the detective, frowning.

'Timmy wouldn't have picked it up if it didn't belong to the thief,' George told him.

'Hallo!' said Ben, who had just arrived, along with Julian, Dick, Anne and Tinker. 'I say – that glove is just like the ones the stewards wear. The Black Mask must have got hold of a complete steward's uniform. I doubt if *that* will help to identify him!'

Mr Daley turned up too. He examined the glove carefully, and then said thoughtfully, 'No, it's *not* a steward's glove. This one is much finer. Feel that material, Vernon – I've never seen one exactly like it. How odd!'

Of course the passengers and their luggage had to be searched again! The Captain hardly knew how to calm Mrs Ivy Flower down – she was telling anyone who would listen that the whole cruise ought to be cancelled!

In the middle of all this confusion, Mischief suddenly appeared. He was chattering excitedly and clutching a little cardboard box.

'Now what have you got, Mischief?' asked Tinker, holding out his hand. 'Come on, give it here, old chap – thanks!'

He opened the box and gave a little cry.

'My word! The Black Mask's visiting cards! This must be his secret supply of them!'

Everyone was rooted to the spot!

'If only we could ask him where he found them.' said Mr Vernon.

'What a brilliant idea!' Dick whispered jokingly. 'Why doesn't he try cross-examining Mischief, then?'

'Shut up!' hissed George. 'I've got an idea. We must give the box back to your monkey, Tinker, and then you tell Mischief to put it back where he found it. Maybe you can get the idea into his head!'

'A good notion!' exclaimed Mr Daley. 'We can at least *try* to identify the Black Mask in that way.'

So a curious little procession formed. Mischief went along the gangways of the ship, carrying the box, and followed by the children, Ben Moore, Mr Vernon and Captain Parker as well as the purser. He made straight for one of the cabins! Once there, he stuffed the box of cards into an open drawer and then turned round, looking pleased with himself.

The children stared at each other. This was Francis Barraclough's cabin! Of course the pianist

99

protested his innocence when he was questioned.

'But *I'm* not the Black Mask!' he cried. 'That wretched monkey just likes playing tricks! Remember how he slipped one of those cards into your own pocket one day, Captain? I'm not the Black Mask any more than you are!'

And that was that for the time being!

The ship's next port of call was to be Syracuse in Sicily. While the *North Wind* headed for this island, the Five, Tinker and Ben met by the lifeboat on the upper deck. They had made this spot their headquarters.

'Let's think it all over carefully,' suggested Julian, 'and try to see just how far we've got! That may help us.'

'Go on, then,' said George. 'Get out your list.'

'I've made some notes too, listing all the things our quarry has stolen since we started on the cruise,' said Julian.

'A quarry who doesn't know we're after him!' said Dick. 'Aha – if he knew the Five were determined to get him he wouldn't be so bold!'

'Honestly, Dick! Don't make me laugh!' said Tinker sarcastically. 'He may be very rash – but you haven't managed to discover who he is yet, have you? The Black Mask's still on the loose!'

'Now, Tinker, you're not being quite fair to your friends!' said Ben. 'They nearly *did* catch him when he was pretending to be a steward. It was just a bit of bad luck that prevented them.'

Tinker went red. 'I was only saying that to tease

George and Dick. They're always so sure of themselves, thinking they're bound to succeed!'

'And they always *have* succeeded, so there!' said loyal little Anne, in her gentle voice.

'With your help, Anne dear,' said George, patting her on the back.

Anne was touched. George never usually made a great show of her feelings! 'Yes,' said the little girl firmly, 'the Five are a really good team! And *I* don't see any reason why we shouldn't catch the Black Mask in the end!'

'Well – this is how things stand!' Julian went on. 'The Black Mask has robbed these people, in the following order – possibly Miss Ping, and certainly Mrs Herrington, Pedro Ruiz, Francis Barraclough, Mr Van Dam, Mr Haziz the hotel manager in Tunis, and then Mr Van Dam again – he really is out of luck, poor fellow! As for out list of suspects, we've crossed off these people – Miss Ping, Pedro Ruiz, Mr Van Dam, Mrs Flower and the Herringtons.'

'Which means,' finished Ben, counting on his fingers, 'that the Black Mask *has* to be either Francis Barraclough, Mr Stone, John Bayley or Luke Martin.'

Tinker, who had been leaning over the rail to look down at the lower deck, happened to see Mr Bayley and Luke pass at that very moment.

'*I* think it's those two,' he muttered. 'They're a funny couple! And I wouldn't be a bit surprised if the Black Mask had an accomplice!'

101

Chapter Eleven

THE PARCEL AND THE IDENTITY BRACELET

Everyone was pleased to arrive at Syracuse in Sicily. They were to stay there for several days, going out on interesting excursions into the countryside. Several of the passengers felt the heat so much that they often preferred to stay on board and have a nice lazy siesta – but the children and the rest of the group of really keen sight-seers wanted to see everything they could!

It didn't look as if the Black Mask was going to do anything while they were anchored off Syracuse, and the passengers began to breathe again.

And then, on the very day when they were due to leave Sicily in the evening, something did happen!

The children had gone into the town on their own that day, with permission from Aunt Fanny, Uncle Quentin and the Professor. They were looking into the shop windows of Syracuse, amused by the contrast between the very modern shops and the old ones, which were full of local colour, bravely holding out against the changes of modern times!

Anne had just bought herself a pretty scarf when George suddenly uttered an exclamation.

'Oh, look!' she said. 'See that man over there?'

'Yes – it's Francis Barraclough!' said Dick. 'And he said he was going to have a siesta!'

'But there he is, keeping close to the wall as he walks along,' said Julian. 'Of course, he could be just wanting to keep in the shade.'

'He does look rather furtive, though,' said Tinker.

'Let's follow him,' said George. 'And whatever you do, Timmy, don't bark!'

They set off, following their suspect at a little distance, but taking care not to lose sight of him.

'Did you see that?' asked Julian. 'He's carrying a parcel all wrapped up ready for the post!'

'And he does seem to be making straight for the post office, too!' said George. 'My goodness – suppose by any chance he *is* the Black Mask, that parcel must contain Mr Ruiz's ruby ring, Mr Van Dam's diamonds, both their wallets, Mrs Herrington's necklace and maybe even Miss Ping's brooch!'

'All we have to do is go and find out!' said Dick.

'Oh, very clever!' said Tinker laughing. 'We just run after him and tell him to unpack his parcel in front of us, do we? It couldn't be simpler!'

His sarcasm was wasted on George – she was already searching for a way of discovering what was really in the parcel the pianist was sending.

'I've got an idea!' she said, stopping suddenly.

'Well, hurry up and tell us!' whispered Julian, seeing Francis Barraclough disappear inside the post office building. 'It'll soon be too late!'

'No, it won't! Follow me!'

And George hurried into a café which had a public telephone in it.

'You have something to eat or drink while I'm phoning,' she told the others. 'I'll be back in a minute!'

In fact it was several minutes before she was back – but then she was looking triumphant!

'I've done it! We'll know what that parcel contains any moment now!' George told her surprised cousins and Tinker.

'But what did you do?' asked Julian.

George smiled. 'Well – of course I didn't give my name!' she said. 'But I phoned the police to tell them I thought there was a bomb in the parcel being handed in at that very moment at the post office – and I gave them the sender's name. There must be all sorts of fuss going on over there now!' she added, pointing to the post office building. They could see it through the café window. 'They'll be hurrying to check that parcel!'

The others looked at her admiringly – you could always count on George and her imagination to

104

solve a problem!

'My goodness, George – I'd *never* have thought of that myself!' said Dick. 'You're amazing!'

'Queen of the detectives – sorry, I mean King!' added Tinker.

In spite of herself, George swelled with pride!

While the others watched for Francis Barraclough to come out, George waited a few minutes and then went back to the public telephone. She rang up the post office, and asked whether a bomb had been found in the suspicious parcel. An angry voice told her that it was a parcel of books on the history of Sicily, which Mr Barraclough was sending to a friend, and that it would be the worse for any hoaxer who went in for a stupid joke like that again!

George didn't wait to hear any more. She stammered an apology and hung up. So Mr Barraclough's parcel hadn't contained anything it shouldn't after all!

Her friends were waiting for her in great excitement.

'Francis Barraclough has just come out of the post office,' said Anne. 'He looked very angry!'

'I'm not surprised!' said George with a rueful grin. 'He had nothing but books in his parcel!'

'So we've drawn a blank yet again,' Julian said.

'Well, never mind! Now I come to think of it, even if he *had* had the jewels, I suppose he couldn't simply have sent them from one country to another so easily – the Customs might have opened the parcel! I'd forgotten that. Well, let's get back to the boat!'

The children found the *North Wind* in a state of turmoil! While they were gone, apparently the Black Mask had struck again! This time he had robbed Mrs Flower. She was complaining bitterly, and for once you couldn't blame her! She owned seven valuable rings with different precious stones – diamond, emerald, sapphire, ruby, topaz, lapis lazuli and aquamarine – and wore one each day of the week. And now they had been stolen!

'Not what I'd call a totally unsatisfactory day,' said George.

'Not for the Black Mask, no!' said Dick, with a grin.

'For us, I meant! You see, while the Black Mask was robbing Mrs Flower, we were following Francis Barraclough – so *he* can't be the Black Mask!'

'In other words,' said Julian, 'we can cross his name off the list too. That leaves just three suspects: Mr Stone, Mr Bayley and Luke Martin!'

The passengers cheered up a little that evening when the *North Wind* entered the Straits of Messina, to go up the east coast of Sicily. Ben pointed out to his young friends what were supposed to be the whirlpool of Charybdis and the rocks of Scylla, both much feared by sailors in the time of the ancient Greeks and Romans. 'But our modern ships

106

have nothing to fear from them, so don't worry!' he said.

The children listened to him with interest – but it had been a tiring day, and they went to bed quite soon after dinner.

When the children woke up next morning, they had arrived at Naples in Italy. They were to spend several days cruising along the Italian coast, and all sorts of excursions had been planned. But George was feeling gloomy.

'We're coming to the last part of the cruise,' she said to the others, 'and we *still* haven't found who our quarry is! I refuse to believe he's cleverer than we are!'

'It looks as if he is, though!' sighed Julian. 'We're nowhere near unmasking him – I'm afraid we shall arrive back at Southampton no wiser than when we left!'

Anne interrupted in her gentle voice. 'I don't agree, Julian!' she said. 'The Five have never failed before! I'm sure George will know how to solve the mystery in time!'

'Woof!' said Timmy, backing her up.

George smiled, feeling pleased. 'Thanks, Anne – I *do* still hope we may succeed! I don't want people saying the Black Mask was too clever for us – especially when we have Tinker and Mischief to back us up too!' she added kindly.

Nothing particular happened during the first day or so of their stay in Italy – but on the third day, when they went on an expedition to Capri, something both dramatic and comical happened!

Miss Ping, smiling and rather embarrassed, appeared wearing the very same brooch she said she had lost while they were seeing Ibiza!

'I found it caught in the lining of the dress I had on that day,' she explained. 'I haven't worn it since! So the Black Mask didn't rob me after all!'

'Well, that's *one* less crime to his account!' whispered Dick.

But he had spoken too soon! On their return from the excursion, poor Miss Ping found she had lost her brooch again – and this time, there was one of the Black Mask's visiting cards in her handbag!

George was furious with herself for not having noticed when the brooch was stolen. However, she said, 'That means we can rule John Bayley out! He stayed on board all afternoon.'

'No, I don't agree,' said Julian. 'It doesn't necessarily show that Mr Stone and Luke Martin are our only suspects now – I know it's thought that the Black Mask operates on his own, but there's really no reason why Bayley and Martin shouldn't be in league together. And look at their initials – B and M, just like the Black Mask! I wonder if *that* has any significance? I think it could be them!'

And something that happened to Anne next day seemed to back him up.

They had left the Bay of Naples and were making for Ostia. Anne was swimming in the pool with the others when the strap of her bathing suit broke. She had another bathing suit in her cabin, so she went to change. She was going along the gangway when she saw a silver identity bracelet lying on the floor, and she picked it up. Its tag bore the name *Luke* engraved on it.

Looking up, Anne saw that she was standing outside the cabin which John Bayley shared with Luke Martin. The little girl was about to knock when she suddenly heard an angry voice on the other side of the door.

'I *told* you to leave the Chinese girl alone,' said John Bayley. 'She was fond of that brooch – and it has so little value, compared to the other jewels. We don't want to risk getting caught for nothing!'

'All right, all right, don't get so angry! I thought it would be funny to play a trick on the girl – and as I had one of your cards on me, I amused myself by slipping it into her bag!'

'What a stupid thing to do! Now listen – in future ...'

Anne didn't wait to hear any more. Much excited, she put the bracelet down outside the cabin and hurried off. The conversation between the two men made it all quite clear – John Bayley was the Black Mask, and Luke Martin was his accomplice!

As soon as Anne had changed her bathing suit she rejoined Julian, Dick, George and Tinker.

'Anne, whatever's the matter?' cried Dick, when

Anne suddenly heard an angry voice on the other side of the door.

'I know who the Black Mask is.' announced Anne.

he saw her. 'You're all pale and trembling!'

'I've got some news!' announced Anne. The others looked expectantly at her. They were standing round the swimming pool, a little way from any other bathers. 'I know who the Black Mask is!' Anne went on.

'Ssh!' George interrupted at once. 'Let's go up to our headquarters by the lifeboat. You can tell us all about it there!'

After Anne had told her story, they were all silent for some time. Timmy didn't move, and even Mischief didn't make a sound.

'Well! That explains everything!' murmured Dick at last. 'So it's John Bayley after all! We've found who the Black Mask is at last!'

'We still have to catch him in the act of stealing something, and get him arrested!' said Julian.

'*And* discover where he's hiding his loot!' added Tinker.

'Yes,' said George thoughtfully. 'John Bayley – yes. He's been very clever, hasn't he? Acting the part of an invalid like that!'

'How can we catch him, though?' said Dick impatiently.

'We must follow him night and day,' said George. 'Knowing who he is makes the whole thing much easier – at least, I hope so!'

George wasn't as enthusiastic as Anne had hoped, but the little girl didn't say anything.

They decided they would take it in turns to split

up into teams and keep watch on John Bayley and Luke Martin. They would work in pairs – Julian and Tinker, Dick and Anne, and George and Timmy. Like that they would surely catch the Black Mask red-handed sooner or later!

Chapter Twelve

THE PROFESSOR'S PAPERS

But something confusing happened on one of their next excursions. They were visiting Rome, and driving along the Appian Way in a coach, when John Bayley suddenly let out an exclamation of dismay.

'My briefcase! I had a briefcase with me, full of documents about stocks and shares – valuable documents! And it's gone! Stolen!'

He had turned very pale and seemed really upset.

'What an actor he is!' whispered Dick to the others. 'Just look at him, making out he's one of his own victims!'

George, who was sitting quite close to Mr Bayley, didn't reply. She was staring at the card the invalid had just found in his pocket, and which he was waving under his neighbours' noses. One of the

Black Mask's visiting cards!

The other passengers in the coach were searched, but nothing turned up.

'You must have been robbed before we got on the coach,' said Mr Daley. He seemed very annoyed!

'Well, I know I had those papers with me when we left the *North Wind*,' said John Bayley. 'It seemed safest to bring them.'

'I say – if we still suspected Mr Stone, this would clear him!' said Dick in an undertone. 'He stayed on board with toothache.'

George was still oddly silent. She didn't say what she was thinking until later, when they were back on board. And then, up in the shadow of the lifeboat, she told the others, 'I don't think John Bayley and Luke Martin are guilty after all!'

Julian, Dick, Anne and Tinker exchanged surprised glances.

'Why . . . but . . .' stammered Anne. 'But I heard Mr Bayley myself, telling Luke Martin off for stealing from Miss Ping and leaving one of his cards in her bag!'

'Exactly!' said George. 'I think that was a very suspicious sort of conversation!'

'What do you mean?'

'Well, listen! You say the two men were talking in very loud voices, Anne?'

'Oh yes! I could hear them quite clearly, without having to strain my ears at all!'

'Don't the rest of you think that was odd?' George went on. 'Do *we* raise *our* voices when we want to discuss something secret? I mean, can you imagine the Black Mask identifying himself in a loud shout?'

'Er – well, no!' said Julian thoughtfully.

'And another thing – if Bayley wanted to tell Luke off, he'd had plenty of opportunities to do it before Anne stopped outside their door!'

'That's true,' said Dick.

'And then there was that identity bracelet with Luke's name on it, right outside the two men's cabin door and ready for Anne to find it!' George went on. 'It sounds to me as if it were all set up!'

'But I *did* hear them saying just what I told you!' Anne insisted.

'I'm sure you did, Anne. But I still think it was a faked conversation. If you ask me, the Black Mask has realised that we're making inquiries, as well as Mr Vernon, and he's trying to send us off on the wrong track!'

'But how?' cried Dick. 'How could he?'

'Well, we still have to find that out!' replied George. She beckoned the others closer, and went on in an undertone, 'Before we all met up here, I checked some of my suspicions – and I got *proof* that Bayley and Martin must be innocent! I asked the ship's barman, and found out that the two men were playing cards in the smoking room at the very moment when Anne heard that revealing conversation between them!'

'But how could they have been?' said Tinker. 'And anyway – if you're right, then we don't have *any* suspects left! If the Black Mask isn't Mrs Flower, or Mr Van Dam, or Miss Ping, or Francis Barraclough, or Pedro Ruiz *or* the Herringtons *or* Mr Stone, nor even Bayley and Martin working as a team – then WHO IS HE?'

'We've still got to find that out, too,' said George gloomily. 'In other words – we have to start from the very beginning again!'

The last place where the *North Wind* was to anchor before sailing back to Southampton was to be Genoa. While the luxury liner was making for that big Italian port, the Five and Tinker, with Ben's help, were doing their best to keep watch on *all* their old suspects! But George realised that this method could succeed only if luck was on their side – and luck definitely seemed to be against them!

It was no real good taking it in turns. George and Timmy or Julian and Dick prowled the ship's gangways in silence by night – and by day Ben, Anne and Tinker joined the hunt. They turned up in the most unlikely places, and they all kept their eyes open – but nothing came of it.

In the end, even George felt discouraged. 'I don't think we'll ever do it!' she whispered to Timmy.

When the *North Wind* came into harbour in the huge port of Genoa, Mr Daley told the passengers that during this last stage of the cruise they would have parties on board and interesting excursions on land.

'To start with, I expect everyone would like to go and see Christopher Columbus's house!' he said.

Of course the usual group of keen sight-seers said yes!

In fact the children were disappointed by Christopher Columbus's house. They had expected a grand building, and instead found a tiny, rickety little place like a roadmender's hut in the very middle of the city. If the walls of this crumbling hovel hadn't been picturesquely covered in ivy it would have looked miserable.

The tourists went back to their coach, not very enthusiastically.

'Now we're going to have a typical Italian meal in the town,' said Mr Daley, 'and then we'll go and see the famous Campo Santo, the biggest cemetery in the world!'

'Oh, what fun!' said Julian gloomily. 'A cemetery! I ask you! That's all we needed!'

Ben, who had overheard him, laughed. 'Well, you'll have to go without me this time,' he told the children. 'I'm giving a big conjuring show on board this evening, and I have to rehearse this afternoon. I hope you'll come and watch the show!'

And Ben left his young friends as soon as lunch was over. The rest of the passengers from the *North Wind* went back to their coach and up the rather hilly road to the distant Campo Santo.

117

To everyone's amazement the two scientists, Uncle Quentin and Professor Hayling, were on this expedition.

'It was very hard work getting them to come!' Aunt Fanny told the children. 'In fact I was only able to get them away from their work because they think this is such an interesting place to visit. The cemetery is full of the tombs of famous people, and they are keen to look at some dates carved on old tombstones.'

The Campo Santo covered three whole hills – such a vast area that it looked like a city itself from a distance, with roads, avenues and gardens. Before they went in through the gateway, Tinker happened to glance at his father. He hadn't paid much attention to Professor Hayling until now – but his jaw dropped open!

'My word!' he said at last. 'How fat my father is! I never noticed!'

'And so is *my* father!' cried George, in astonishment.

Aunt Fanny started to laugh. 'Don't worry, children! It wasn't all the spaghetti we had for lunch – they haven't really put on a lot of weight, they're just following Mr Van Dam's example!'

George and Tinker still didn't understand, so Aunt Fanny explained, smiling, 'Mr Van Dam kept his precious stones in a canvas belt round his waist – well, Professor Hayling and your father are doing the same with their precious papers!

Knowing the Black Mask is on board our ship, they don't trust the purser's safe on the *North Wind* – they thought they'd rather bring their papers with them while we were out, and their pockets are stuffed full of scientific documents!'

'Oh, how silly!' cried George in her usual forthright way. 'The Black Mask wouldn't want to steal their old papers!'

'Don't be so sure,' said Aunt Fanny. 'Those *old papers*, as you call them, are very valuable! They contain the secret details of a very important formula. Your father and Professor Hayling have been at work on it together.'

'Ha, ha!' Dick laughed. 'I'm not a bit surprised! Uncle Quentin and Professor Hayling just wouldn't have been happy on this cruise without their work!'

The party went into the huge cemetery, following a great many other tourists, and a guide came to help them.

'This way, ladies and gentlemen. Please follow me!' he said in good English, with an Italian accent.

It was very hot, and the children were beginning to wish they had opted for a siesta instead. 'We *must* keep our eyes open,' George repeated for about the tenth time.

'We *are*, aren't we?' said Dick, a bit crossly.

'Come on!' cried Tinker suddenly. 'Help! I can see my father taking off his jacket because of the heat – he's quite forgotten his pockets are full of important papers!'

'Yes, we'd better go and keep close to him,' said Julian. 'Suppose the Black Mask –'

But the boy didn't have time to finish what he was saying! At that very moment an extraordinary thing happened. Tinker's father was passing an old tomb with a statue of a bronze angel with outspread wings on top of it. Suddenly the angel seemed to split in two – and a masked figure dropped on Professor Hayling's back!

The two men rolled over on the ground, and before the watchers had recovered from their surprise, the scientist's attacker ran away among the tombs, clutching Professor Hayling's jacket. He was gone in a moment.

'The Black Mask – quick, after him!' cried George. 'He can't escape us now! Catch him!'

But that was easier said than done! The Black Mask was quick on his feet. He could be seen reappearing briefly, running among the tombs and monuments and swerving to throw his pursuers off. Soon they didn't know *where* to look for him! The passengers from the *North Wind* were running here and there among the tombs, chasing him and jumping on anything that seemed to be moving. There were some amusing moments! Seeing a shadow on his left, Mr Van Dam pounced on Mr Stone – just as Mr Stone was getting ready to pounce on the Dutchman!

The attacker ran away among the tombs, clutching Professor Hayling's jacket.

The passengers were running here and there among the tombs.

It was all maddening for George! Only Timmy could have caught the real Black Mask – but unfortunately dogs weren't allowed inside the cemetery, and Timmy had had to stay behind in the coach!

The comical chase came to an end when they realised the Black Mask had definitely got away. Julian found Professor Hayling's coat behind a marble vault. Of course its pockets were empty – their precious contents had been stolen.

'And we don't have any idea who did it!' muttered George. '*Any* of the passengers could have slipped away on the quiet and come back in a mask. We can't keep watch on everyone at once!'

Professor Hayling was calling the thief some awful names! Uncle Quentin was furious, too. When they were back on the *North Wind* the two scientists went to see Captain Parker to complain.

George couldn't help smiling as she told the others, 'They just wouldn't come out of their scientific dreams until Professor Hayling was attacked! It's almost funny, isn't it?'

But really the children were very gloomy. Even Timmy seemed to be sulking. George said it was because he understood – the brave dog had lost his chance of catching the Black Mask by the seat of his trousers when they made him stay in the coach!

However, the children cheered up that evening as they watched the conjuring show Ben Moore was putting on for his attentive audience. The young man was smiling and handsome in a dark blue dinner jacket. Carefully and deliberately, he put on a pair of white gloves and started manipulating playing cards and balls with amazing dexsterity! Next, he did some of his new tricks, including an unexpected one for which he said he needed Timmy's help.

Timmy was very surprised to see pigeons fly out from between his paws and perch on top of his head. But if it bothered him he didn't show it! Ben was George's friend, so he was Timmy's friend too – and Ben had told Timmy not to move, so he didn't.

The audience applauded like mad.

At the end of the show Julian, Dick, George, Anne and Tinker congratulated Ben, and then they went to bed. But George kept on waking up and thinking of the theft of Professor Hayling's papers. She had dark rings under her eyes next morning – but her eyes themselves were shining! And directly after breakfast she said solemnly to her cousins and Tinker, 'Let's go up to our HQ! I've got something to tell you!'

Once they were on the upper deck by the lifeboat, George started talking at once. 'Tinker, now that those papers have been stolen from your father we must act fast,' she said. 'We *must* get the Black Mask arrested, and make him give back everything he's stolen!'

Julian looked at her in surprise. 'Get him

arrested?' he exclaimed. 'But we don't even know who he is yet!'

'That's why we must act fast! We only have two days left. I suppose the problem's been on all your minds long enough for you to have worked out who our quarry must be! Well, let's exchange our ideas.'

'Myself, I've got *no* idea!' said Tinker. 'To start with there were so many suspects we didn't know which to pick – and now there aren't any at all. It's crazy! I don't know what to think!'

'I'm the same as Tinker,' confessed Anne. '*I've* no idea either!'

George turned to Julian and Dick. 'What about you two?' she asked.

Dick rubbed his chin. 'Well, I *have* got an idea, but I don't really think much of it,' he said. 'What about Mr Daley the purser? No one's thought of suspecting him – but he's been on all the excursions, and he could send Mr Vernon off on a false trail if he wanted to.'

George shook her head. 'No,' she said. 'We can leave the purser out of it. Except when he's taking parties of passengers on land, he's always on the ship – so he can't be the Black Mask, who has committed so many crimes on land. Have *you* got any ideas, Julian?'

The tall, fair boy seemed to hesitate. 'Well, yes,' he said at last. 'I can only see one way to explain how the Black Mask can run rings round everyone – he's *several* people!'

'How do you mean?' asked Dick.

'Well, suppose the name 'Black Mask' really covers a small group of criminals operating in turn?'

'In that case it could be *any* of the passengers,' said Tinker.

'That's right.'

George shook her head. She didn't seem convinced. 'If you ask me,' she said, 'having a gang makes things complicated. Sooner or later the members of the gang quarrel, and then it breaks up. Or else they give each other away! Well, the Black Mask has been at work for quite a long time, and there's been no hint of any trouble. I'm sure he's on his own!'

'I bet *you've* got an idea, though, George!' said Dick. 'And a better one than ours – haven't you?'

George smiled rather sadly. 'Yes, I *have* got an idea,' she said simply. 'I think Ben Moore is the Black Mask!'

Chapter Thirteen

UNMASKING THE BLACK MASK

There was a stunned silence. Then Julian, Dick, Anne and Tinker all started talking at once.

'But that's impossible! Ben is our friend – he's a really good sort! He's so nice! George, you're mad!'

George interrupted them.

'So nice?' she said. 'How do you know? Our friend – well, that's what *he* says!'

'But he's been helping us!' Dick pointed out.

'Let's say he's been letting us take him into our confidence! He knows just what we've been doing – and he's had a better chance than anyone else to frustrate our plans! He must have been laughing like anything!'

'But, George, what reasons have you got to suspect Ben?' cried Julian.

George rose to her feet and looked at her cousins and Tinker. Then she said, seriously, 'Well, listen!

Quite a lot of things struck me about him, though I didn't actually notice at the time. There's his name, Ben Moore – you remember how you suggested Bayley and Martin have the same initials as the words Black Mask, Julian? Well, so does Ben's name! And then, he made out he was our friend – so although he went on all the expeditions during which the Black Mask struck, we never thought of listing him among our suspects! There were other things too: the white glove lost by the man pretending to be the steward, who stole Mr Van Dam's jewels, was a very fine and most unusual one – well, you saw Ben using gloves like that while he was doing his magic tricks yesterday evening!'

Stunned, the others listened.

'And another thing!' George went on. 'When the Black Mask made his earlier attempt to get into the Dutch diamond merchant's cabin, do you remember how Timmy went after the thief? And what happened?' George paused before going on. 'We saw Timmy come back with Ben. Ben said he'd called to Timmy as the dog was passing, so Timmy stopped chasing the Black Mask. There was something I didn't like about that – once I've given Timmy an order he doesn't stop for *anyone*, even a friend! No, it was really like this: I told Timmy to go after the man, and Timmy *did* – and he caught him. But as it was Ben, Timmy didn't actually attack him, knowing he was a friend of ours. I expect he thought it was all just a game. And after that, all

127

Ben had to do was take off his jacket and mask!'

'Good gracious – that would explain everything!' cried Tinker.

'Wait a minute – I haven't finished! It isn't surprising we weren't getting anywhere much with our inquiries – Ben was laughing up his sleeve at us! But about the nastiest trick he played was making Anne think Bayley and Martin were the men we were after.'

'Yes – how did he do it?' asked Anne.

'Well – I think he stole Luke Martin's identity bracelet and left it in full view outside the cabin door when he knew the cabin was empty. No one passing that way could help seeing the bracelet, and naturally anyone who did would stop. And so along you came, Anne. I expect Ben was watching from a doorway. As soon as he saw you were going to knock on the cabin door he projected his voice to imitate the voices of the two men. Last night I remembered he was a ventriloquist as well as a conjurer. That's come in very useful for him!'

'Well, he certainly fooled us all!' said Dick angrily. 'And what are we going to do now? How do we unmask him?'

'I thought of that last night, too,' said George.

'George, you're amazing!' said Julian.

His cousin looked pleased. She went on, 'This is my idea – listen to what we're going to do ...'

*　　*　　*

A little later the children went up to Ben Moore, apparently as friendly as ever.

'Hallo!' said Ben. 'How are you all today? Has your father got his papers back yet, Tinker? I really am sorry about that!'

'Oh, it doesn't matter,' said Tinker.

'That's right,' said George. 'We'll tell you a secret, Ben – the papers the Black Mask stole from Professor Hayling yesterday aren't all that important! Tinker's father is clever, you know. His *really* important formulas are written on very thin paper and hidden in a secret place – you'll never guess where! They're in the hollow heel of the Professor's left shoe!'

'Oh, George!' said Tinker reproachfully. 'You shouldn't have said that – it's a secret.'

'Oh, I only told Ben – that doesn't count!' said George airily. 'Now, how about a swim?'

The children went away, leaving Ben alone. A smile appeared on the conjurer's lips.

'Well, well!' he murmured. 'His left shoe! Thanks for the information, you young innocents!'

That evening Professor Hayling went to his cabin the same as usual, after a long talk with Uncle Quentin after dinner. He undressed, had a shower, and lay down. Soon he was fast asleep.

It was about one in the morning, and the Professor was still asleep, when a shadowy figure gently opened his door and went over to his clothes. The visitor, who wore a black mask to hide

The visitor picked up one shoe and retreated, very quietly

'You wretched child,' the jewel thief said. 'But for you...'

his face, picked up one shoe and retreated, very quietly.

Suddenly the silence of the ship was broken. The Five, Tinker, Uncle Quentin and Aunt Fanny, the Captain, Mr Daley and Mr Vernon came bursting out of the neighbouring cabins.

Before he even knew what was happening, the Black Mask – who had meant to copy the stolen document he thought he was carrying off and then put it back in its place – found himself caught! He was powerless. His black mask was taken off.

'Well done, George!' cried Dick. 'You were right! It *is* Ben Moore, and he fell into your trap!'

The jewel thief looked at George, eyes flashing angrily. 'You wretched child!' he said. 'But for you ...!'

He had defied everyone for so long – and now he had been captured by a group of children!

As he was being taken away the passengers, roused by all the noise, came out of their cabins wanting to hear the extraordinary story. They all exclaimed in amazement, and everyone wanted to congratulate the Five and Tinker.

But George still wasn't satisifed. She heard next morning that Ben had refused to say where his loot was hidden, and yet another thorough search of the boat had found nothing. She called a council of her cousins and Tinker. 'It's still up to us!' she said. 'We'll very soon be back in Southampton, and then the police will come on board. We want to find the

131

stolen jewels before they do, don't we? *And* Professor Hayling's papers!'

'Yes, we must certainly do our best,' said Julian, Dick, Anne and Tinker.

But there was so little time for them to find the valuables the Black Mask had stolen – would they manage it?

To start with, they worked out all the parts of the ship to which Ben could have had access. Mrs Flower, who was much nicer to them now, and obviously hoped her rings would be found, offered her help. So did the Herringtons, Miss Ping, Mr Stone and Francis Barraclough. Mr Bayley offered them a big reward if they could only find his briefcase.

In fact, everyone was doing all they could – but though they searched and searched, nothing at all turned up that day.

'We only have this evening and most of tomorrow left!' sighed Anne. 'Tomorrow evening we reach Southampton and go back to Kirrin!'

'Don't let's give up,' said Tinker. 'We must go on searching!'

Evening came, and the children were still baffled.

'Oh well!' said Dick. 'We must go on looking tomorrow – did you know there's to be a fireworks display this evening?'

'Good!' cried George. 'I'd love to see some fireworks!'

Forgetting their problem, the children decided they must really make the most of their last night at sea. Only Anne was a little sad when she thought of their 'friend' Ben. She had trusted him – and he'd tricked them.

'That's life, Anne. Just forget it!' Dick advised her wisely. 'You'll learn as you get older!'

That evening all the passengers met for dinner, which was a particularly good meal. Everyone seemed more relaxed now that the Black Mask had been arrested. He was to be handed over to the English police next day. Even Mrs Ivy Flower was being quite nice to everyone!

'Here's to our young detectives!' said Captain Parker, raising his glass to the children. 'Thanks to them, this eventful cruise of ours has ended happily!'

Poor Mr Vernon, the unsuccessful shipboard detective, applauded like everyone else. Aunt Fanny looked proud and happy. But her husband and Professor Hayling weren't paying attention to anything but their own conversation!

'And now the fireworks!' said Mr Daley the purser. 'Two of the ship's officers are going to set them off from a little boat, far enough from the *North Wind* for you all to enjoy the show without any danger of fireworks falling on you. I suggest you all go up on deck!'

While the boat carrying the fireworks went off into the night, the passengers settled comfortably in deck chairs or leaned over the rail.

'Let's go up to our HQ!' suggested Julian. 'We ought to have a good view from the upper deck.'

'All right,' agreed the others.

It was not long before the first rocket rose into the calm night air. It burst in a shower of sparks, and fell back into the sea, crackling gently.

Perched on Tinker's shoulder, Mischief narrowed his eyes and uttered worried little sounds. He didn't seem happy!

Absorbed in watching the fireworks, the children took no notice of the little monkey. Another rocket rose to the sky. This time there was a series of bangs as it disintegrated in a sheaf of multi-coloured sparks.

Really frightened now, Mischief buried his little face in Tinker's neck. Tinker patted him reassuringly.

'Don't worry, Mischief! Keep still.'

The fireworks went on and on, lighting up the sea and the sky. The show ended with a huge set-piece, accompanied by what sounded like real cannon-shots.

Mischief was absolutely terrified. He lost his head! Jumping down on the deck, he disappeared into the dark, squealing with fear.

'Oh, bother!' said Tinker. 'I should have put him on his leash, but he's usually so good that I didn't think of it.'

'Let's go and catch him!' said Dick. 'The

firework show's over, anyway.'

The Five and Tinker made for the ladder down to the lower deck. Mischief must have gone that way!

'I expect he's trying to shelter in our cabin, and we'll find him outside the door,' Tinker told Julian and Dick.

But the little monkey wasn't outside the boys' cabin. The children spent the next hour searching and searching, asking everyone they met, but nobody had seen Mischief. They just couldn't find him!

At last Tinker gave up hope. 'Poor Mischief – I think he must have fallen overboard,' he said sadly.

But George had a sudden inspiration. 'Why didn't I think of it before?' she cried. 'Tinker, let's get the cushion Mischief sleeps on and give it to Timmy to sniff!'

Timmy took a good sniff at the cushion. 'Now, seek!' said George. 'Good Timmy, good dog – seek Mischief! Seek!'

Timmy didn't need to be told twice! He went off at such a pace that George only just had time to catch hold of his collar.

'Hey, not so fast!' she cried. 'Wait for us, Timmy!'

First of all, Timmy went back to the lower deck – and then up to the children's headquarters on the upper deck.

'This is all very well,' grumbled Dick, 'but he's

135

just taking us back to where we started from! That won't get us anywhere!'

'You leave Timmy alone,' said George. 'He knows what he's doing.'

Timmy stopped beside the lifeboat, just where the children used to meet. Then he stood up and put his front paws on the lifeboat itself – and then put his head right in under the tarpaulin that covered it and snuffled hard.

'Woof!' he said.

A frightened little cry answered him. Quickly, Tinker and George pushed back the tarpaulin, and saw Mischief crouching in the bottom of the boat. When Tinker put his hand out, the monkey disappeared into the box of emergency rations – he had managed to open it!

'Naughty boy!' said Tinker. 'Come on out, Mischief!' He put his arm out to try and grab Mischief – and upset a jar of drinking water. But it didn't make the sloshing sound they would have expected. There was a metallic ringing noise instead.

The children looked inquiringly at each other.

'What can be in it?' cried George. Taking the top off the jar, she tipped its contents out on the deck. A heap of jewels fell at her feet!

'Mr Van Dam's precious stones! Mrs Herrington's necklace! Pedro Ruiz's ruby ring – Mr Barraclough's watch – Mrs Flower's rings and Miss Ping's brooch! They're all here,' she cried.

Julian picked up a biscuit tin and opened that too. He found several wallets stolen from the passengers, *and* Professor Hayling's papers.

'Well, fancy that!' cried Dick, thrilled. 'Timmy has found the hiding place where the Black Mask put his loot!'

'It was partly Mischief's discovery,' said George.

'But it was your idea to send Timmy to look for him,' said Tinker, ready to give credit where credit was due.

Really delighted, the children picked up the treasures they had found and went off to hand them over to the Captain. Captain Parker was very surprised, and so were the purser and Mr Vernon!

'Well, children, you never cease to amaze me!' said the Captain. 'Thanks to you, I shan't be reprimanded by the company – and tomorrow we hand Ben Moore over to the police. Now we can give the passengers back their stolen property!'

It was an extraordinary scene! Everyone wanted to thank the Five, congratulate them and reward them! Timmy was offered so many biscuits that it was a wonder he didn't get indigestion – but then he was a very sensible dog!

The *North Wind* came into Southampton Water in triumph. The police and the press, who had heard the news of all the excitement by radio, were there waiting. Press cameras flashed as the Five walked down the gangplank off the ship, followed by Tinker and Mischief.

Once all the passengers were ashore Ben Moore, alias the Black Mask, appeared. He kept his head down and tried not to let the reporters get a good look at him. Ben wasn't so proud of himself any more!

That day the grateful passengers invited the children, Aunt Fanny and Uncle Quentin and Professor Hayling to a special celebration meal before they went back to Kirrin. It was a happy occasion. They were soon all to part – 'But we shall never forget what you did for us, dear children. You and that darling doggie!' said a gushing voice.

George could hardly help laughing. The speaker was none other than Mrs Ivy Flower!

'Well, I call that even more extraordinary than our own achievements – or the Black Mask's!' she whispered to her cousins and Tinker. 'Fancy seeing our Bad Fairy turn into a nice, kind, grateful person! This cruise has certainly been full of unexpected things!'

'Woof!' agreed Timmy.

And everybody burst out laughing!

THE FAMOUS FIVE AND THE STATELY HOMES GANG

The Five are pleased to be spending another holiday at Kirrin Cottage, the scene of many of their adventures. And this holiday proves to be as exciting as all the others, from the moment they set off on their shiny new bicycles!

KNIGHT BOOKS

THE FAMOUS FIVE AND THE MYSTERY OF THE EMERALDS

A summer holiday camping on Kirrin Island is the prospect in store for the Five, and they're eagerly looking forward to exploring the island.

But when George overhears a couple of crooks planning a jewel robbery, the Famous Five set off on a dangerous and thrilling trail.

KNIGHT BOOKS

THE FAMOUS FIVE AND THE MISSING CHEETAH

Arriving for two weeks' stay at Big Hollow, the children are delighted to discover that Tinker has a new friend – a cheetah!

But twenty-four hours later, Attila the cheetah has been kidnapped, and his abductors threaten to shoot him unless they're given the formula for a new, top-secret fuel.

KNIGHT BOOKS

THE FAMOUS FIVE AND THE GOLDEN GALLEON

A wrecked yacht, The Golden Galleon, is washed up near Kirrin Island, with a cargo of gold ingots. The Famous Five discover it was used by some bank robbers for their get-away, and when the gold vanishes overnight the Five embark on an exciting treasure hunt.

KNIGHT BOOKS

THE FAMOUS FIVE GO ON TELEVISION

A holiday treat is even more exciting than expected when the Five are invited to play themselves in a television series.

Shooting is disturbed, however, by some sudden and mysterious disappearances. The children suspect that a kidnapper is at work. But who, and why?

KNIGHT BOOKS

More exciting adventures from Knight Books

All these books are available at your local bookshop or newsagent, or can be ordered direct from the publisher. Just tick the titles you want and fill in the form below.

Price and availability subject to change with notice.

Hodder & Stoughton Paperbacks, P.O. Box 11, Falmouth, Cornwall.

Please send cheque or postal order, and allow the following for postage and packing:

U.K. – 55p for one book, plus 22p for the second book, and 14p for each additional book ordered up to a £1.75 maximum.

B.F.P.O. and EIRE – 55p for the first book, plus 22p for the second book, and 14p per copy for the next 7 books, 8p per book thereafter.

OTHER OVERSEAS CUSTOMERS – £1.00 for the first book, plus 25p per copy for each additional books.

Name ....

Address ....

....